POISON IN THE AIR

T0037139

POISON IN THE AIR

BY JABBOUR DOUAIHY

TRANSLATED BY PAULA HAYDAR

Interlink Books

An imprint of Interlink Publishing Group, Inc.
Northampton, Massachusetts

First published in 2024 by

Interlink Books
An imprint of Interlink Publishing Group, Inc.
46 Crosby Street Northampton, Massachusetts 01060
www.interlinkbooks.com

Copyright © Jabbour Douaihy, 2021, 2023
Translation copyright © Paula Haydar, 2023

Originally published in Arabic as *Summun fī al-hawā'* in 2021 by Dar Al-Saqi,
Beirut, Lebanon

All rights reserved. No part of this publication may be reproduced, stored in a
retrieval system or transmitted, in any form or by any means, without the prior
written permission of the publisher.

ISBN 978-1-62371-754-4

Library of Congress Control Number: 2023941628
LC record available at: https://lccn.loc.gov/2023941628

Printed and bound in the United States of America

"My hunger, which savors not the fruits of this earth
Finds in their absence a most gratifying taste"

Stéphane Mallarmé

THE BOOK OF EXODUS

THE WOMAN LETS her body sink into a wicker armchair that we had in our home for many years. She's wearing a sleeveless polka dot dress that reveals her pale white arms. Her head is tilted, her hair black and wavy. Hanging on the wall, just above her head, is a picture of General De Gaulle. He's standing in front of a large microphone, addressing a gathering of soldiers. To her left, a boy with damp hair is seated on a tall, backless stool, wearing shorts that may no longer be suitable for his age. His feet are dangling above the floor. In the middle of them lies a dog, curled up and peacefully asleep on the floor. From a distance, the world appears suspended, still, as in some paintings of saints surrounded by domestic animals amid luxuriant gardens— paintings created by anonymous artists that Syrian peddlers would holler at us to purchase as they meandered through our alleyways, carrying massive sacks on their backs filled with towels and undergarments. If one steps closer to get a better look at the picture hanging from a piece of twine, they'll find an indecipherable horror in the woman's eyes, as if, having reached age forty-five, she's just discovered the enormity of human destiny. The boy's face shows clear signs of some other worry, and even the commander of the Free France Forces appears to be angry. Only the dog seems to be enjoying the tranquility that follows lunch during the scorching summer season.

As for the adolescent, that's me, and the woman is my paternal aunt. The dog, Fox, belonged to our neighbor the hunter. The photographer had propped up my aunt's sagging shoulders and straightened her head before calling out some silly expression I didn't respond to. I didn't smile. That photographer used to go door to door, just like the *malban* candy seller or the copper pot bleacher. He'd stand at our front door, saying nothing, not even hello. He'd light the flash in our faces and then wait for us to invite him in. When he came back with the picture two days later, we made a wooden frame for it and hung it on the wall where it had been taken—above the wicker chair—my aunt's favorite place to sit.

My mother and aunt usually stayed at home all day while my father left for the cobbler shop that effused the aroma of leather and glue. During school vacations I would go with him. He forbade me from playing with the sharpened leather knives. I watched how he took the foot measurements, drew the patterns, cut, and glued. Men wearing their keffiyeh and *egal* came from faraway places to seek him out. They placed orders for knee-high boots they would display with pride when they mounted horses or wrapped themselves in heavy winter abayas.

During the school holidays my mother would go shopping in the Tripoli souqs. I would sit with my semi-paralyzed aunt who'd been unable to articulate clearly ever since her stroke. Saliva would drool from her mouth, but she couldn't feel it. She rarely spoke, and if she did, she slurred her words, with the exception of some lines of poetry she'd memorized during her school days. Those she would sing out at least once a day without mispronouncing a single letter.

We weren't alone, my aunt and I, because the front door was always open, summer and winter. If any sort of mishap took place, the neighbors would come running to our rescue, like one time when the dog bit my bare leg. I let out a shriek and a burly man scooped me up and threw me over his shoulder. With my head dangling near his butt, I could hear him farting with every step. I was distracted from my pain watching everyone walking upside down, until we reached the school clinic. The nun in the white habit stuck me with a tetanus shot as a preventative against rabies. From that day on I loathed being around domestic animals. Fox would come to the door, stick his nose inside, and then saunter off.

We lived in a crowded neighborhood where doors were never shut until bedtime. Each hour had its sounds. Night came with the croaking of frogs and the distant howling of foxes. Cars would wake us up thanks to drivers beeping their horns for no reason. We had one neighbor who started slurping straight arak the moment he got out of bed in the morning. He'd spit on the floor inside his own house, holler the "Our Father" and "Hail Mary," and go around looking for some excuse to beat his wife, who would shout curses back at him—though much less skillfully than her husband—before throwing her arms up over her head for protection. I'd get dressed in a hurry so I could watch the scene before the school bus arrived; despite his cheeks blazing red with anger, he was cautious with his blows. We never saw any bruises or blood. I worried his tasseled tarbush, which shook with each strike, might fall off his head, before some armed men came to break up his morning calisthenics. My mother would say that his wife loved him, that she took care of him even when he became senile and no longer recognized her and accused her of trying to rob him. She shaved his beard for him, placed the tarbush on his head, tipping it slightly to the right, and sat him in a chair near the front door. She'd step back and then correct some detail in his appearance. She wanted him to look like a man with full dignity, the way she'd always imagined him to be but never actually saw in real life. When passersby greeted him, he smiled without recognizing them.

After the morning clamor, I headed to school, where we were forbidden from speaking in Arabic under threat of punishment. We perfected our writing in Arabic and French, memorized poems, sketched color drawings of the human heart with all its pipes and ventricles and atriums, just as we drew from memory a map of the Normandy region and its major cities.

My classmates could not bear to see me sitting and reading out on the playground during noon recess. I read in the lavatory and in the cafeteria while eating my lunch. One of them would snatch my book, *A Tale of Two Cities* by Charles Dickens, and fling it up in the air where it would get caught in the branches of the poplar tree. Then they'd try to bring it down by throwing rocks at it before skedaddling from the angry recess monitor. I nominated myself to run unopposed as the "library supervisor." Every day I would meander through that chamber where the daylight streamed in through the windows and glimmered against the wood of the bookshelves. It was then that I formed a connection between expensive wood and books. Then one day the principal came to me and said, "Here you go. The key to the library. I will never find anyone to take better care of it than you."

My heart started pounding. I began bringing books home with me and would read them to my aunt, who sighed at certain passages as though remembering one of the many romantic chapters of her youth. When I sat down beside her, I was struck by the smell of the products she used to straighten her hair—a smell that always made me gag. I read to her on Saturdays, our day off. Poems she loved, or tales of chivalry. I read to her after I got back from the early morning slaughter fest.

On goat days, the butcher carried out the work by himself, and on calf days, two men shared the job: the butcher and his nephew. We could hear the tethered animal on the sidewalk lowing from the first hours of dawn. The church bells and the lowing of the calf, who people said could sense what was coming, woke us up. I'd rush out with one of my buddies, not wanting to miss anything. The butcher would send us to the sidewalk across the road so we wouldn't get splattered with blood. Severing the calf's neck was easy. One slice from one jugular to the other. The two men would calm the calf down. They'd rub his neck tenderly so his muscles would relax and then suddenly attack him from behind with a sharp blow before he tensed up. Slaughtering him while he was terrified would make his meat tough and hard for the customers to chew. His eyes stayed open, gazing in our direction across the road, making us feel a bit guilty for not doing anything to rescue him. They skinned the calf carefully. They cut him down the middle and his guts poured onto the ground. I didn't look away from the faces of the calm and carefree butchers, like the faces of tailors or basket weavers hunched over their workbench, while the blood splashed onto their clothes. One of them grimaced only if his knife got stuck between two bones.

They'd shoo the dogs away with some vulgar expressions and finish peeling off the meat. The owner of the butchered animal would start shouting to customers, and his neighbor—a butcher like himself, less than twenty meters away—would start responding and "slashing" the price. The *zajal* rhymes would circulate, with insinuations and outright claims that so-and-so's meat was "local" while the other's was imported. One time the argument became so heated it came to profanities and the brandishing of sharp cleavers. We ran home, and after a little while we heard a groaning sound akin to a calf's lowing. We found out later that the fat butcher we'd been watching that morning fell victim to a knifing from his adversary that spilled his guts. I saw him that night in a dream with his stomach ripped open, shouting to his customers about his fresh slaughter. The man died before reaching the hospital.

I followed the butchers secretly, being careful not to let my mother know. I am an only child in this life, my parents having failed to give me the gift of a brother or sister. My mother worried about every single thing I did. She worried about my eyes getting tired in the semi-darkness in which I turned the pages of my books. She warned me not to swim naked in the river at the start of spring—as she'd heard from some snitches—and against fraternizing with the "troublemakers," as she called them. That meant all the boys in our neighborhood and the adjacent neighborhoods too. She warned me against staying alone in my room, where "harmful thoughts" might come to me, and against walking barefoot. Everything I enjoyed doing scared her. The mere sight of me content and cheerful probably worried her. Even my always being ranked first in my class on every type of school exam worried her, not because she didn't want me to be happy or succeed but because, in her heart, she felt she had to prevent me from wearing myself out. I was her only child, true, but in time I began to feel that wasn't the reason for her constant panic over me. My guess was right, because behind those countless fears of hers was an uneasiness of another sort, whose reason I happened to discover one day by chance.

There was a man in his thirties residing in our neighborhood who lived with his sister and worked as a math teacher. He had a hard time getting his students to listen to him. They'd scream and quarrel with each other. Infuriated, he would sit silently at his desk until the kids settled down, and if they didn't, he'd pick up his things, leave the classroom, and never come back. He was the only one in a wide radius around our house who wore a suit and tie every day. My mother referred to herself as "auntie" to him, affectionately and also as an indication that he was related to her. She'd invite him in for coffee whenever he walked arrogantly past our house, as if on tiptoes. He never accepted the invitation, but one time, having learned of my passion for reading, he insisted that I come visit him at his house. I was amazed by the number of mirrors hanging on the walls inside his house, and by his sister, who let out a burst of laughter the moment she saw me and laughed again at other moments when there was no call for excitement. He gave me a book about the history of the Phoenician kings of Tyre, and we made plans to get together again to talk about the book.

That turned out to be our only meeting, because two days later, on a humid night when sleeping is sticky and sweat drips off bodies, just when the fifty-year-old woman known for chanting dirges for the town's dead—gratis—was entertaining the neighbors with love songs like "O you who have wounded my heart/This wound really hurts" ("*Ya jaarha galbi wil jurhi yi'limni*"), a sharp cry resounded from my mother's relative's house. The air was so unbearably suffocating, something was bound to explode. The math teacher had grabbed hold of a cane made of oak that might have belonged to his father and started swinging it at all the mirrors in his house. He broke everything that could be broken before the neighbors converged on him and stripped him of the cane. They shepherded him the next morning to the psychiatric hospital, where it was said he kept up his elegant appearance but quit his former habit of peering at himself in the mirror and tweezing his eyebrows dozens of times a day.

I got the gist of that story by chance. My friend's father was sitting at a low table eating dinner one evening. His wife disappeared into the kitchen and came back carrying the arak and tabbouleh while the conversation between them continued. I was in the bedroom helping their son with his French homework, since word had gotten around in the neighborhood that I was fluent in French. His parents were discussing the incident with the math teacher without realizing I was listening to them on the other side of the wall.

"Some minds just can't bear a lot of knowledge," said the husband.

He went on to mention various individuals who'd gone overboard with their studies and how their behavior became disturbed, like the one who shunned marriage or the one who mocked the mystery of the immaculate conception and who used to talk to himself in a loud voice and wave his hands around...

"What's education got to do with it?" his wife interrupted. "That one's mother is from the Sabbagh family."

They debated about education and heredity, but the woman appeared to win the round when she rattled off a sequence of names of people who were eccentric or even mentally deranged, all descending either on the father's side or the mother's side from the Sabbagh family. She topped it off by saying, "There's one at Dayr al-Salib Asylum where they took our neighbor, the math teacher."

My mother is from the Sabbagh family.

She got displaced along with us from one house to another. I don't remember much more than a few fleeting memories of our first house in Midan Square where I was born. The smell of the fish seller who used to come to the house with his basket brimming with Sultan Ibrahim fish every Friday. The sound of intermittent gunshots as my father stood at the door with the daylight streaming in, saying something I didn't understand that made my mother gasp and made me start crying so hard I nearly fainted, though I didn't know why. Our stay in that house was no longer "appropriate." In other words, we were no longer safe, because that neighborhood was not *our* neighborhood. We moved all our furniture and belongings to this second house in batches, and then my aunt moved in with us.

Likewise, our stay next door to the math teacher who was obsessed with mirrors didn't last long either, because the government suddenly decided to wipe the entire neighborhood off the map. The prime minister, an urban planner who didn't last long in office, made a visit to our town. He insisted on going through our neighborhood with his entourage on foot. Horrified by the jumble of houses and residents, he asked in an audible voice, "How can a man sleep with his wife in this place?"

Two months later, he issued a decree annexing seventy lots for the purpose of establishing a secondary school on the site. To maximize the square footage on the ground, the architect planned the construction of four complexes. Each two-story building had eight lecture halls and between the buildings were playing fields and green spaces. Some of the statistics collected by the Appropriations Department at the Ministry of Public Works included perhaps one hundred names of property owners and tenants, meaning nearly four hundred people living within an area no more than two thousand square meters. Apparently, the compensation had been generous, and people started tearing their own houses down to get the money as quickly as possible.

Two police officers came to serve us with an official notice to vacate the premises. My mother grabbed her flowerpots and the Bible. My father grabbed the Brylcreem he used to shine his hair, the record player, and his records, which were primarily by Mohammed Abdel Wahab. He gathered up his cobbler gear and moved it to the new house because it was no longer safe for him to go to his cobbler shop in the next neighborhood. My father was clean and stylish and never worked without donning his apron. He didn't show any traces of his occupation except the black stain around his right thumb index finger, because he washed his hands vigorously with soap several times a day.

And so, we got displaced a second time and ended up at a third house. This time my father wanted us to live near his family and his clan. I did not find "our folks" to be any more sympathetic to us, but my father was always saying, "Whatever befalls us befalls them too."

For my part, I grabbed my books and the picture of me with my aunt, and I slid a compass into my pocket that I liked to find north with a hundred times a day. A relative had given it to me after he retired from the Merchant Marines. At age fifteen I began suffering from acne, "teenager pimples," as they call it, and I started experiencing bouts of sadness that sometimes pushed me to the brink of tears, especially on Sundays or at sunset. I took pride in the fact that those intimate heartaches came on without warning, as if there was a vessel within me that filled up drop by drop until it overflowed. I wasn't like the other neighborhood kids or my schoolmates who showed signs of misery for merely running out of pocket money and not being able to go see *The Siege of Troy* at the cinema, or for getting rejected by some girl they were chasing. Those were mundane matters that were of no concern to me. I was sad because I was sad. This difficult disposition of mine emerged at our new house, amid the smell of leather and glue that moved in with us when my father started "stretching" shoes at home.

Whenever my parents went to visit one of our relatives, I would take advantage of their absence to go hide in my room. I'd pull the covers up over my head and let out loud sobs that my aunt couldn't hear, or I'd sit out on the balcony hugging a cotton-filled pillow to my chest while fixing my gaze without blinking at the high mountains, which had a bluish hue.

My father had gone ahead of us to the neighborhood by himself, so he could survey the house's location before putting down the rent, which was higher than some other houses. In his mind, the house was protected on the southern side, the direction danger might come from if the situation got worse. And he chose a house behind another lofty two-story house built of sturdy stone. To shield us. And truly, the living room teemed with neighbors my father greeted with a smile the moment any gunfire was heard nearby. The first of the refugees was a fat girl who came tumbling in out of breath and pounding her chest with her fist as she implored Saint Elias to strike down our enemies with his sword, before proceeding to sprinkle holy water over everyone's head. Opening our door to anyone who asked was our sole contribution to the defense of our relatives. My father was no good with guns, and all I could manage to do was imagine scenarios, before falling asleep at night, in which I masterminded schemes to ambush our enemies and catch them by surprise, clamp them in the jaws of a pincer, and bring down the largest number of victims possible. My mind eagerly planned out the massacre, but my zeal waned the moment we overtook our enemies and started killing them. So I'd resume waylaying them in dark alleys and surprising them all over again from rooftops until I fell asleep.

Matters didn't go sour all at once. Guns were kept concealed in the pockets of baggy overcoats or kept oiled and ready by front doors. There weren't any casualties, but there was poison in the air. A palpable desire to spill blood. Meanwhile, the circle started closing in on me before everyone else because I was an only child and was fragile. If something bad were to happen to me, my mother would die of worry and my father wouldn't last long after that in a life that would have little meaning without us. He nodded in agreement over that possibility. He'd place the anvil between his legs, pick up the shoe with his left hand, and pound it with the hammer in his right, the thin nails he held in his mouth making it impossible for him to talk. He'd gesture with his head that he would leave this world. Yes, he didn't know how, but he would catch up with us if I got killed and my mother followed after me. I felt he was just cajoling us. My disabled aunt would be left all alone with no one to look after her. They worried about me, but I wasn't the least bit troubled about the things that made them worry, as though there was a thick glass wall between me and danger. I could see it, but it couldn't get to me.

A while later I heard someone say that the school bus route had become unsafe. Preparing for the worst, I started stuffing my school bag every day with volumes that I'd surreptitiously pulled from the library shelves. That was before I was forced to return the key to the principal when we got permanently dismissed from our classes, all

19

so we could go home to our civil war whose reasons we couldn't fathom at the time, and which, when we finally got out of that war years later, we realized were petty. From the moment I became aware of that fight, I knew it was a simple equation: They were there and we were here and there was no way around fighting each other.

Then a sunny morning came, after a night of gusty rain, when the sound of a loud explosion rose up from where our house was. A bomb had landed amid the morning calm outside our window. The shrapnel destroyed all my mother's expensive kitchenware, glasses and teacups she'd had since her wedding, and it also shook my father's faith in our house's location. It was unclear where the rocket had been launched from, and the neighbors stopped taking cover behind our walls. They did continue seeking me out, however, to write letters for them to send to their relatives in the diaspora.

"What do you want from them?" I would ask one of them, and he'd say, "Just hellos and this and that."

I would embellish the letter with poetic phrases about emigration and how love for the homeland was "a killer." Then I'd add some innuendos about unemployment and poverty. Replies would come from Sydney or Caracas with money they hadn't asked for tucked inside. I also went into detail describing the tensions in the town and predicting the worst. And that's what finally happened. We had our first casualty at last.

The young victim was one of ours. He was riding a bicycle when he was shot, so he kept going while bearing the pain until he reached the bridge where he fell to his death into the dried-up river that autumn day. Presumably he died from the fall into the riverbed because the bullet only hit his arm. That was the prelude to all evil. Everyone was mobilized. My mother came out looking for me while I was trying to find the place where they'd laid out the body. I was hoping for a comparable scene—hundreds had given up the spirit in my books—King Henry IV was stabbed to death with a dagger; Romeo drank poison and died. I'd read quick descriptions but had never seen a dead body. Even my paternal grandfather didn't let me near him the day he'd gone onto the next life, and all the cobblers and their apprentices attended the funeral.

I snuck over to the place where two men were washing the bicyclist's body. They had wrapped his arm and plugged up the hole in his head with a piece of cloth. I said to myself, if I remove it, I could see inside his skull. I volunteered to wrap my arms around him so the two men could dress him in a nicely ironed white shirt. I questioned that, though, pointing out that God created us naked, so why should we return to Him in clothing of our own making? The men scoffed at me while I propped up the dead man's head on my shoulder. When I let him back down on the bed so they could put his trousers on, he let out a moan. Shocked, I let him slip from my hands. One of the men made the sign of the cross. We couldn't find a black tie, but it didn't really matter since neither I nor the two men knew how to tie one anyway. We hurried to finish up before he became stiff. We laid him out on a bed, and I sat there staring at his smooth, wrinkle-free face and his color, which gradually turned from light green to white. His fingernails were dirty. He had been a car mechanic. They took his wristwatch but left his ring to be buried with him because his fingers were swollen.

On my way back home, I sniffed my clothes. I pulled my shirt collar up to my nose trying to detect the smell of death. I couldn't keep my promise not to expose myself to danger. I kept rushing out to examine the dead as soon as I heard any news of casualties. I discovered all the varied shades of pallor on their faces, and I noticed that there was never much money in their pockets to speak of.

I was distracted from my inner sorrows while keeping company with the dead, the wounded, and the suffering, but during long lulls in the fighting, my sadness would return. Some days the sun rose and set without a single report of gunfire or casualties, and so I would withdraw back into myself again, go back to my books, and sit despondently on the balcony, facing the mountains sketched behind the clouds, quoting the poet's lines aloud:

> I am the prince of darkness—the widower—the inconsolable
> My only star died out
> The only sun that rises over me is the sun of black despair*

When the fighting resumed, I would head towards the sound of gunfire, whereas other people ran away from it.

---

* Translator's note: This appears to be a loose quote from de Nerval's "El Desdichado"—the author's Arabic paraphrase of these lines in French:
> Je suis le Ténébreux, - le Veuf, - l'Inconsolé,
> Le Prince d'Aquitaine à la Tour abolie:
> Ma seule Etoile est morte, - et mon luth constellé
> Porte le Soleil noir de la Mélancolie.

I didn't want to miss anything. I wanted to be right in the middle of what was happening, there the moment one of them fell to the ground so I could try to drag him out and treat his wounds. I'd come back home with blood all over my shirt. My parents would give me hell and my aunt would also join in as best she could, accusing me of trying to get myself killed. I'd promise to stop, but then go running the next day to bandage the wounded and listen to the cries of those in pain.

Then quiet came, despite no one having asked for it, since both sides still had the ability and desire to keep fighting. A strange, undeclared ceasefire entered its third week. Time started to drag on heavily as though life no longer had any purpose. Nothing exciting, nothing to look forward to. My mother resumed her visits with girlfriends and my father went back to listening to Abdel Wahab's "When Evening Comes" while hammering shoe leather. I meandered around the perimeter of our neighborhood like a drifting spirit, looming at the borders of the adjacent quarter to scout out what was happening over there. I'd peer at the new school where migrants—like us—from other neighborhoods were squatting, fearing for their lives, before any students ever stepped foot in it. The windows got broken and the walls got sooty from the fires the squatters ignited inside.

We would fight during the day and be gripped by insomnia at night until, at noon, the bombs started falling on us. They fell from the sky, killing and wounding many people, and smoke and fires ensued. Our house was spared, but my father hadn't figured 81 mm mortars into his calculations when he rented that sturdy house with its red-tiled roof. We found out that the rocket that had destroyed my mother's kitchen was merely a test shot. Up to that point, taking caution had been a horizontal thing; we feared sniper fire. But after that, vertical danger got added to the list. From time to time, we would look up, though we didn't know how we would protect ourselves from that.

They bombed us at night the next time, so no casualties were reported, as though the darkness swallowed up their bombs. In the morning, my father went out, headed to a mountain village whose inhabitants he told us were very peaceful, and returned in the evening with orders for us to move out.

"Third time's the charm."

So he said.

That was our exodus from Egypt. Our last and final displacement from the place of our birth.

I would go ahead of him with my mother and aunt, and he would join us later after figuring out what to do with our furniture. We kept pace with my disabled aunt as we dragged our luggage. We crossed the river on a rickety wooden walkway, and when our feet landed on steady ground again and we climbed up a hill, I stopped to catch my breath and take in the view of the town. Then I howled like a prairie wolf from the depths of my soul, sending cries of joy to the heavens that were like the ululations of women at a loved one's wedding, as if I'd made it out alive or emerged victorious from a battle to the death. I emerged into the world having grown a pair of wings. I could almost fly. I had my books with me and had no idea what to expect, but I was excited about my future. As usual, my mother worried about my sudden mood swing. She hugged me close to her chest and kissed me on the head to calm me down. At that moment my aunt remembered a line of poetry by Elia Abu Madi. She recited it eloquently, standing in the shade of a poplar tree.

O you who complains though nothing ails you
Be beautiful, and see the world around you beautiful

We kept going in the direction of the main road, hoping to find a taxi to take us to our mountain destination. I took out my compass and shook it, not knowing where I wanted it to lead me, while two Hawker Hunter planes circled over the town tracing two white lines of smoke behind them. We heard a deep explosion before turning to walk away.

THE PRACTICE OF LOVE AND WRITING

MY FATHER CHOSE a quiet place for us to live that I think held some sweet romantic memories for him, a village whose townspeople knew the secret to producing sweet wine, which they sold and rarely drank themselves. All the villagers who emigrated away from the town settled in the same neighborhood in the suburbs of Springfield, Illinois, where they had their own school, church, and restaurants. They say that there are more of their townspeople across the seas than there are living here, 1,700 meters above sea level. They use riding animals, preferably mules, for transportation to their mountainside orchards. They are skilled at quarrying stones into square blocks, out of which they carve huge mortars for tenderizing meat. They lean in to drink from a marble deer's head that spouts water into a font in the middle of the square, and they kneel with outstretched hands to beg for the intercessions of the two saints of their church—two Roman army officers who were beheaded when it was discovered that they had joined the Christian faith.

I brought along a provision of books for myself, which was fortunate because my prediction came true. I wouldn't find a friend or neighbor who could supply me in times of need with something to quench my constant thirst for reading. I was always careful not to exhaust my stock of books. This was an involuntary sentiment, a constant feeling of lack that stuck with me and is still stuck with me, making me avoid at all costs not having something to keep me company during my final days on this earth. Whenever I imagine myself in retirement, I see myself alone or in the company of a silent woman who's upset at the world while I sit looking through a wide window at springtime scenery, on a wicker rocking chair, tortured more by emptiness and the battle against the passage of time than concerns about death. Even before I turned twenty, I began resorting to stopping midway through a book I was enchanted with, leaving the second half for another distant day I feared would come when I wouldn't find any books around.

During that period, news reached us of our stubborn hometown that was still eagerly pursuing its war. Modern weapons came onto the scene; more people were killed. Their names would trickle to us with people who'd recently emerged from that inferno of vengeance. They would come back into our memories for a moment and my mother would let out a fleeting sigh over their squandered youth. After a short time, their faces would vanish from our memories and go out like a flame. News reached us of Fox's demise when he crossed the demarcation line between the two neighborhoods. He'd been heading toward the secondary school in a seeming attempt to go back to his old neighborhood, to his home next door to ours. Bullets rained down on him from the other side. They fired at him with their semi-automatic rifles as though practicing on a moving target. They brought down the old dog who was dragging himself along, no longer good for hunting. We also heard about the death of our former neighbor with the Turkish *hamidi* tarboosh.

"He died a natural death," my father said, meaning that he hadn't been shot. I said to myself that his wife, whom he used to beat up, would be wearing black mourning clothes for him a long time.

"Until it's her turn to die," my mother said.

I made peace with myself in those high mountains. My depression disappeared. I'd left it back in my hometown imprisoned inside my aunt's trunk of clothes that my father couldn't figure out how to carry with him to our new residence. In the end he was forced to go back and get it because my aunt wouldn't stop her griping and muffled moaning. She rarely left the house, not having any girlfriends, and spent her days between her clothes and her makeup. She took her time bathing every day and would put on a new dress and spend over an hour carefully checking every aspect of her fine appearance. She used to call me over—before she had her stroke and became half paralyzed—to sit beside her while she powdered her cheeks with pink blush and removed the little hairs from inside her nostrils with tiny scissors. After she got sick, I knew what she wanted as she sat in front of her mirror with her body tipping to the right, which I helped her straighten only for it to slump back again a little later. One by one, I'd hand her various beauty tools or products, and when she finished, she'd crack a smile—something between satisfaction and pain—and only answer the one question that always haunted me:

"I'll die if I don't do this."

I learned from my aunt that getting dressed up was something a woman does for herself, not for others. As a reward, she'd plant a long kiss on my forehead as if saying farewell before standing up and leaning on me so we could walk gingerly to the living room, where she sat until lunchtime on the wicker lounge chair where we'd had our picture taken with Fox sleeping at our feet.

My paternal aunt was the pillar of our house. My mother favored her but with conflicting emotions. I'd find them whispering together, plotting about the goings on in the world and about the neighbors in particular. After she became ill, my mother tried to keep a smile while telling her the gossip. She called her to lunch every day with great respect and she took care of her every need when she grew unable to manage on her own. She rebuked any criticisms against her but took advantage of her absence to suddenly describe her—as if she'd gotten tired of defending her—as a *bint hawa*, a "girl of passion"—my mother's polite term for a whore. The difference between the two women was stark. My mother was one of those "village" women. She'd dropped out of school early and displayed some feminine charms early in her youth—a wiggle as she walked or a certain hairstyle. She married a young tradesman who at the time had a cobbler shop he'd inherited from his father with four assistants working under him. Word had gone around that her family had met with another young man from the town, and her parents spread a rumor that their daughter was going to marry him. And so, my father panicked and couldn't stop himself from kidnapping her. She had a baby with him and immediately after that relinquished all claim to femininity and genteel manners. She devoted herself entirely to serving us—my father and me. I think it's possible to classify my mother among the last of a dying breed of women. As for my aunt's story, that's a long one. She won a beauty contest in her youth in one of the summer resort towns, and she sparkled like a shooting star. All the suitors became infatuated with her. A man who was very rich but advanced in age won her over by catering to her every whim and inundating her with presents.

"He slept with me only two times," she informed me, treating me like a grownup from the time I turned fifteen. Her glory days lasted less than a year. Her husband died and left her a huge inheritance. Her trousseau was still new—dresses she'd never worn and shoes she'd never tried on. She stuffed them into some suitcases and took off to Brazil. There she found lots of men who invited her to dance parties. *Estrella* magazine in Sao Puolo even called her "the Lebanese Bella." She married a rich widowed cattle rancher.

"That one could never have enough."

She divorced him and got married again in Colombia to a man who quickly joined the armed revolution. He was the only one she said she loved with all her heart, maybe because he was the one who took off on her. She came back to Beirut and from there to Cairo, where she appeared in some small cinematic roles. She married a stage actor.

"Poor guy," she said about him. He had a heart attack in the middle of playing the role of Majnun Layla. It was clear that her sole talent was in her beauty and the ease

31

with which she reeled men in and didn't turn her nose up when they gave her a share of their money. She'd made the acquaintance of Asmahan, Layla Murad, and Youssef Wehbe, whose voice enchanted her, and whenever she was feeling down, she would reminisce about all the men who loved her. She didn't love; she was loved. She counted them off on her fingers by their first names. Khalil, Fernando, Augusto, Abdelfattah … She suggested I write her story.

"You won't find another story like it. Publish it and make a name for yourself out of it. It'll sell a lot. Believe me."

Her ailment crippled her and silenced her.

The day she moved into our house, I was present for the opening of her suitcases. My mother helped her while jealously eyeing her jewelry and undergarments. My aunt supported us financially with paper currency—large bills she pulled out of nowhere and tucked into my father's hand once a week. We were her only kin, and my father's trade no longer made ends meet. It got "hit" by ready-made shoe stores, so my aunt volunteered to pay my tuition and our rent, and she did not acknowledge any heir other than me. Her constant aim, which was always being delayed, was to go with me to the bank to switch her private account into a joint account in both our names to make it easy for me to get her money after she died, and no one would be able to contest it.

In this new estrangement of ours, my aunt's condition improved due to the dry climate, and she started taking a few steps on her own from her chair to the dinner table. The place was peaceful, the sun warm, the trees shady, the water ice-cold, and the days predictable. Only one man with white hair and a slender build broke up the routine.

From the early morning he'd weave through the square in front of the church, going in every direction. He'd speak aloud to the water fountain, tirelessly introducing himself and his noble origins, then carry a rose to his mother's grave, where he'd spend the other half of his day kneeling and weeping.

As for myself, my emotions settled down. I strolled along paths where I could smell the aroma of goats, picked wild mulberries wherever I found them, and carved on tree trunks the names of poets who were cursed and died in the prime of their youth. One time, I wrote out my will in beautiful script. I asked to be cremated and for my ashes to be sprinkled into nature with the music of the Kyrie Eleison playing in the background. And I bequeathed all my possessions to the neuropsychiatric hospital that cared for the mentally ill—the sages of this world as I called them. I stuffed the paper into a Coke bottle and threw it into a small gushing spring that streamed down into the valley.

Then something happened that I never expected up in those high mountains among simple apple orchardists and stone cutters. My father's good reputation followed him after he brought his supply of Italian leather and everything he needed for crafting it, which had been reduced from a spacious workshop filled with tables and shelves and workers to an anvil, an apron, and a set of tools that could fit into one box that he carried with him anywhere he went. The villagers where we'd settled made durable shoes tailor-made for the fields and snow, and the women wore rugged, sturdy shoes. One day, a young woman came to see my father. I didn't look up to see her face when she came in because I was sitting next to my father, lulled by the smells

33

of his craft and the movements of his hands. I was bent over my book, so what I saw was a soft white foot stretched forward for my father to trace a line around with his pencil to take a measurement. I knew the possessor of that foot must be a stranger to the village, and it was also evident from her carefully manicured nails painted with red polish.

I struck up a friendship with her when I volunteered to deliver her new shoes. I turned the beautiful handiwork over in my hands, imitating my father by blowing on the leather and shining them carefully. At her house I met her sister, who was her equal in age and beauty. One of them asked me how I liked living there and I found myself saying in all eloquence and romanticism:

"This village is best described as a beautiful exile for broken souls running from the burdens of life and yearning for an impossible peace."

The one with the shoes' eyes lit up. She detected in my words the scent of an intimate friend. She invited me to sit and join her for her afternoon coffee. The resemblance between the two sisters was identical. They denied they were twins in the beginning, but it didn't take long for them to admit it. They justified their denial by saying that sameness and the idea of twins diminished their attractiveness. One wore her hair shoulder length while the other cut it short like a boy, and one sister would not wear a dress unless the other was wearing pants. Likewise, the one who came out of her mother's womb minutes before the other voluntarily declared herself the firstborn, but they always went everywhere together and competed with each other in seductiveness, which made matters difficult for them and anyone they befriended. Their parents gave them similar names, ones with just two syllables as had started to become popular at that time. More like cat names. They were renting a furnished house for the summer; they'd gotten bored after not finding any young men to fulfill their constant desire for romance. They mocked the males of the village because they loved to plant pear trees called "mule brain pears," were skilled at building terraces out of white stone and searched for a woman they could mount at night, who cooked bulghur wheat and tomatoes for them during the day and raw kibbeh on Sundays.

The girls took no interest in knowing how the boys, whose blunt advances they flatly turned down, had ended up in that place. Even its own inhabitants said, "Nobody can live in these barren mountains except the native monkeys."

I took interest, and at the start of their competition over me, I tried to dazzle them with stories, some of which I'd read, and the rest stories I made up about the people of that place. They derived their origins from monks and hermits who lived in the plains, in the Levant, and believed that with the imminent approach of the first millennium, the end of the world was at hand. They climbed into the trees to make an abode for themselves. They stood up on pillars and preached to the voracious crowds about miracles, they settled in deserts and tied iron chains to their necks, they ate grass and insects, then they climbed up the mountains for protection, and the idea of Judgement Day near at hand continued to hound them until they forgot about it and went back to eking out a living in this beautiful place. And I drew some other tidbits from history books for my stories, like the ancestors of those peasants having been pummeled by a catapult from King Qalawun's army and their besiegement in a cave where they died of thirst. All that because of their collaboration with the Crusaders. Then someone came along who betrayed them, led the enemy to their hideout, and they were smitten by a curse that lasted generations.

The girls grew tired of my fantastical stories. What they'd been looking for was some excitement in the here and now. They were two sisters free for companionship and frivolity, and so I responded to their offer and listened to their secrets. I'd lend my ear to each one individually while not being able to choose between the two until the more forward and enticing one won me over in the end. The one with the short hair. The other sister was resigned to her lot, with no hard feelings, as though she was used to her sister winning the boy contest. Her only condition was that I should tell her in detail everything that transpired between us whenever she left the house so we could be alone, or we went on a stroll through the woods, just the two of us. We'd lie down in the shade of an umbrella pine, exchange some hot kisses, and listen to the trickling water or the howling of jackals.

The other sister wanted to hear the story from me, not her sister. When I'd tell her the next day what happened between us, she'd close her eyes to listen. I'd distort the facts a little bit in order to hide that I was a beginner at sexual matters. It's correct to say that I was still a virgin. My romantic adventures in the town where I was born had been limited to a surprise attack from our fat neighbor who used to pray to Saint Elias for us to have victory over our enemies on the eastern side of town. She cornered me one day in the kitchen, next to the refrigerator.

She revealed her breasts and pummeled me with kisses and lots of sighing and moaning. Nothing could free me from her but the sound of my aunt calling for me after she'd heard the noise we were making and thought an intruder had broken into the house. The rest amounted to a few exchanges of promising glances, as happened to me with that brunette who used to stare at me. It was those green eyes of hers against the dark tone of her skin that made her beautiful.. People said she dished out her attentions to everybody from in front of her mother's fabric and notions shop where she worked all day long. Her image used to come to me in the evening. I'd bring her into my readings, set her down beside the characters in my stories. One morning she came across that street of hers and I was convinced that I was going to succeed in living out my silent desire for her. I picked up on her voice before I saw her, and that was the very first time I got to hear what she sounded like.She was screaming in her mother's face, complaining to her about some matter related to the store. She had a man's voice, with a heavy accent and harsh vocabulary. The bark of an angry man. I turned around and headed back home after my short-lived dream of her came crashing down, and I banished her from the kingdom of my imagination.

With the twin sisters, I fell for the first time, in one go, deep into the cauldron of love, all the way up to my head. The sister who liked me would instruct me without words in the art of kissing and touching, of taking it slowly and satiating the senses. She would appease my ardor and guide me along the map of her body to what she found pleasurable. She took mastery over me, ruled over my emotions and aroused me until I shuddered and sent myself violently, the way she liked it, until she trembled and squealed in delight. I would quiet her down because her sister might be listening from behind the door. No, I was certain she was there peering through the keyhole and savoring the sound of us inside that house, where I never saw a father or mother or brother throughout the days we spent there together. We continued to engross ourselves in our daily exchanges, and the thought of asking them about their family situation slipped my mind.

After some shy introductions, we entered a stage of fights that she unexpectedly started one day. I came close to her for a kiss and she slapped me across the face. She attempted to keep the impulse in check, as if we were on a swiftly moving carriage pulled by two horses, and she suddenly decided to yank on the reins.. I stopped at that point, confused. She laughed in my face and wiggled her way away from me, so I went after her and cornered her. We had a pillow fight and then toppled to the floor all in a tangle. We'd fight during the day and make up at night. Fighting became our game. The game of denial and delay, to make the reunion all the sweeter. She'd lock herself up in her room and tell me to stay outside for a whole hour before I could win her. I'd sit waiting in the parlor, either overcome with boredom or forced by desire to subdue myself. I'd get up to leave before the end of the hour but the moment I stepped towards the front door, I would hear her bedroom door open so she could chase after me and bring me back to the game. She admitted to me that she was spying on me from inside her room, through the keyhole. Seeing me nervous turned her on. My facial expressions, my repeatedly checking the time on my wristwatch, my body's movements, my eyes looking every which way. She'd pull me by the hand, toppling us onto the living room sofa, because she didn't like beds and bedrooms and never took off all her clothes. Every time we got together her sister would disappear like magic, by previous arrangement or some signal from her sister. The house would transform into a stage. We were content with the warm light of sundown that came in through the windows as we acted out, during that obscure moment between light and darkness, roles of characters I recalled from my books that I would assign to each of us. I'd wrap a black cloth around my head like a pirate to be Arab Othello brandishing his pointed dagger, and she'd play Desdemona, the infatuated Venetian beauty. I'd walk crooked like a cripple like Quasimodo ringing the bells of Notre Dame cathedral, and she would dance like Esmerelda the Gypsy. After she protested these sad roles, I played Don Quixote in pursuit of Dulcinea while she wrapped herself in the sheer white curtain like a dream that is difficult to achieve ever since I told her that she didn't exist, that she was an invention of the Knight of the Sorrowful Countenance. After that I became a clown sticking my tongue out at the setting sun and laughing for no reason. We traded clothes once. She was a man in my tight pants, and I was a woman in her loose-fitting dress. We acted out our roles in earnest and whoever started to laugh failed the test. Then one day I brought a notebook and pen with me and stood before her pretending to start writing and announcing my new role.

"I am the princess's scribe and biographer, ready to set down everything she says and does, hour by hour."

She grabbed the pen from my hand and said, "Eureka! You will write to me every day!"

I protested saying that I was only a reader and knew nothing about writing. She used her tactics to persuade me—she sat in my lap, wrapped her arms around me, whispered in my ear, bit me, scratched me, and kissed me on the neck until we reached a binding agreement that required me to write her one letter each day I desired to be with her. One full page in which I would pour my feelings about what was transpiring between us or about any matter that came to mind.

"Let yourself go," she said to me. From then on, whenever I knocked at the door, before letting me in she'd ask if I'd brought the letter with me. And I'd hand it over before we surrendered to our games.

Those were my first writings other than the compositions that my schoolteachers liked and would read out loud to the whole class. At home, I had to bear the anxious looks from my mother, worried as usual about my feverish behavior that was plain to see. She warned me not to commit the thing she feared, which was some obscure action she never specified so I might know if I had done it or not. She would tell me by way of an opposite example using reverse psychology, the story of her younger sister, my maternal aunt, whom I have no recollection of except for the image of a smiling face, brimming with happiness, someone who joked with everyone and showered everyone with kisses. The earth cracked open and swallowed her up one day. She left the house waving goodbye and never came back. A tidbit of her secret was uncovered when it was rumored a few days later that a man had also disappeared—a husband and father who had been seen secretly talking with her a few times. They took off to Africa where they worked in commerce. My mother says that his family gives her dirty looks and his wife curses her and her whole family in a loud voice whenever they run into each other in the street or at the grocery store.

Here I was now, all grown up, and my mother no longer knew how to take care of me. She decided to give in to a fate that left her humbly begging God not to be harsh. I sat to write at the table where my father worked. He fashioned shoes while I fashioned sentences. The images would come to me. My physical desire for that short-haired girl sparked them into being. I wrote for one specific reader and always felt that I was drinking an unquenchable pleasure from a water spring that never dried up. Phrases came to me from every direction. Any banal detail would be transformed by my pen into passionate words that my friend would read in bed at night and tuck under her pillow before falling asleep. She'd sleep on them, as she put it, adding that my words aroused feelings in her that had been dormant for a long time.

Forty-two letters. I was nineteen years old when I wrote that daily "homework." I'm not sure where I plucked them out from, or how I, with limited familiarity with the Arabic language, managed to create them. It must have been my youthful imagination that breathed life into them, infusing them with flavor and blossoms. I've forgotten all of it except some phrases or single words that got stuck in my memory, as if some other person had written them or as if I'd composed them in a state of epiphany, of ecstasy. From where did I get the ability to

41

invent the kinds of words the world was filled with during that purple-hued summer, the summer of the two sisters, the summer whose elixir we drank daily, with those hostile flowers. And what were those hostile flowers? What was that nightly balcony music that had the power to curb an adolescent's endless selfishness? Likewise, I would ask myself, what pleasure will my friend find when I write to her in one of my letters.

"The dead peer at what is around them. They can't believe our emotion. The village idiot drinks from the well and he is struck with longing for lands he hasn't left behind."

I wrote with unparalleled ease. The words spilled out of me. I drank without stopping from the chaos of emotions and things in a world with no order. It struck me with its possibilities, so with words I would open up a tiny window of meaning in it that slammed shut ever so quickly. In those letters of mine was an illuminating essence that got snuffed out when we turned the page and moved to Beirut. I spent a unique summer in which I threw myself into the arms of a young woman who I might have invented out of snippets from my readings. I was incapable or even refused to get to know her as she really was, and I would never know if she existed. She contributed to that by being stingy about revealing details of her life to me, to keep her story wrapped in the fog of enticement.

It seemed as though that amazing summer would never end. Its emotions were too strong for me to ever forget, and its ghosts floated over my head, and then, with no warning, it just came to an end. The curtain dropped down suddenly without the final scene.

The two sisters disappeared from the town in the morning. A taxi arrived from Beirut and sped off with them and all their belongings. I headed to their house at sundown as usual, ready for a new evening rendezvous to seesaw us between the games of foreplay and the effusive literary imaginings. The landlord informed me that they'd paid the remainder of the rent. She asked them before they left if they wanted to reserve the house for next summer and one of them told her that they would not be coming back there again after that day.

I stood there subdued, contemplating my situation. The woman tried to comfort me. She told me that I was a handsome young man and could have something better any time I wanted, and she didn't like their behavior anyway.

Her words were not convincing. As soon as I was alone, I cried like I'd never cried since my depression waned. I went overboard screaming and moaning until I'd emptied out all that was inside me. Then I realized that I had been making myself cry so sadness could come over me and I could have feelings that suited a painful moment of separation such as this. Still sobbing, I got rid of everything that reminded me of her. A picture of her in a bathing suit, or a sphynx souvenir she'd given me. In return I gave her the compass that a relative who was a sailor had given me. And I gave her some books, but only ones that I had duplicate copies of. I don't think she really liked reading, though.

I was a young man, and forgetting was easy for me. I used to take solace from a quote I'd come across at a young age in some book whose title I don't even remember, and through which I understood a week after that sudden separation that love is a disease, but it's the kind that can be cured. The reality was that when I entered her world and got to know her sister, her house, and the village perched on the cliff's edge, I was crafting a story out of all of that to comfort myself, a narrative that no one could steal from me. It lived with me for a while before the clamor of the city sucked me in and I was stricken with forgetfulness.

A warm autumn with its various gradations of orange colors helped me walk my way to the end of the summer. My aunt and I were enjoying it down a road surrounded by poplar and pine trees. I carried a book with me, held it open in my right hand, and propped up my aunt with my left. I read to her with my sweetest voice, finally resuming this activity with her after having been preoccupied with those romantic training exercises. I made sure to walk delicately beside my aunt with her little white umbrella with the embroidered edge, which she'd taken out from her trousseau for the first time despite the sun's gentle rays. I imagined us in an impressionist watercolor painting of an English countryside. All we were missing was the ancient castle that usually appears in the horizon of such paintings, along with men on horses and hunting dogs pursuing foxes and deer in a most beautiful patch of land. I stopped sometimes to throw a rock at a walnut tree whose fruits I then peeled, blackening my fingers, and fed to my aunt, who had not been unaware of the company I was keeping the prior months. Then, after a bout of complete silence that befell her as usual the moment we left the house, she suddenly began reciting aloud with perfect pronunciation what seemed to be a summation of my summertime story and a synopsis of her own romantic escapades as well:

"Don't trust women and don't believe their promises.

Their satisfaction and their displeasure are hanging from their chests."*

With the onset of the rains that kept us cooped up indoors around the fireplace where my mother and my aunt would be lulled to sleep by the warmth, the place became arid, and my parents, who had grown bored in their turn with living in depressing towns—especially my mother, who had spent the summer all alone with no acquaintances—decided to resume our nomadic life and go to Beirut.

---

* These lines allude to a poem quoted in the introduction (frame story) to *The Thousand and One Nights* (*Alf Layla wa Layla*) in which King Shahriyar, having been maligned by his wife's infidelities, takes out his revenge on all women by marrying one after another only to have them executed the morning after their wedding night. Here the narrator's aunt quotes a witty variation on the crass opening lines of that poem which loosely translate as: Don't place your trust in women or believe their promises//Their satisfaction and their displeasure are connected to their vaginas.

THE GENIE BOTTLE OF THE CITY

WE MOVED TO a place on the fourth floor of an antiquat-
ed building with no elevator. Etched in stone over the
entrance it said, "Dominion belongs to God by proxy of
the Haj Abdel Rahman Agency." Our apartment did not
overlook the main street but rather had a view of some
other buildings that also had their backs turned to General
Wegan Street, which ran parallel to ours. Strange odors
wafted over to us there whenever a northerly wind blew in,
and the five daily calls to prayer reached us from Abu Bakr
Al-Siddiq mosque. I wasn't really involved in domestic
matters except for running some intermittent errands and
looking after my aunt, who would summon me to read to
her from my books as I tried to flee. All that was asked
of me was to devote myself to my university studies after
having breezed through my humanities division baccalau-
reate (and helped the two candidates seated near me to
boot!) despite my involuntary absence from school.

I answered the call of the city. The city that I'd only
visited once before with my father when I was ten years old.

We'd come all the way from far up north to see a renowned doctor who told us as he bent over a scientific journal that I'd contracted meningitis. He said it in French, "*méningite*." I was not the least bit concerned about my illness. Since my early youth, I'd been leaving all worries and concerns to my parents. My mother wrapped her arms around me while I pressed my nose against the window of the taxi on our way back to our hometown and started observing the sidewalks, the traffic officer, and a blind man being guided by a dog as he sold lottery tickets on the corner.

That obscure call made me jump out of bed each morning and speed off like a rocket. I tumbled down the stairs finishing my breakfast *kaak* and buttoning my jacket. No job was waiting for me, nor was any friend I'd planned to meet up with either. I went out into the streets alone just to go out into the streets. To not miss anything that might have transpired while I was away. I came home late at night when my parents and my aunt were already asleep even though I was sure that my mother didn't close her eyes until she heard me shut the door behind me, after which I could sense her turn onto her right side and fall into a peaceful slumber.

No one in that poor Beiruti neighborhood knew my father. Out of need, boredom, and his conviction that a man's presence at home was a burden, my father began making his way around to the various shoe factories in the area. It didn't take much to convince the manager at Red Shoe, the first place he stopped, that he was a talented craftsman. The manager hired him as a supervisor at a pretty good salary, and so my father started going to work on a daily basis. He took care choosing the leather and designing various shoe styles. His taste was classical, his ideal model English

Oxfords. He supervised the gluing and nailing, pushed the workers hard, but lovingly. And he, too, would get tired and go to bed early, sometimes even before my mother and aunt headed to their beds.

On her part and in order to inject some excitement into her and my aunt's life, my mother tried to put together a circle of friends that reminded her of her neighbors back in the town where she was born. She started inviting the women who lived in the building to morning coffee. The first to accept her invitation was an Armenian woman who undoubtedly shared some of the same feelings of estrangement as my mother. Her husband was a famous car mechanic. The first visit wasn't of much use, between my aunt's silence and the neighbor's broken Arabic, until a Beiruti woman joined the group with her thick accent. Whenever I lingered at home, hers was the only voice I'd hear. She monopolized the conversation. She was the local, and the listeners were strangers. She would teach them in minute detail the recipe for Lebanese-style *mulukhiyeh* or *kibbeh arnabiyeh* with the seven citrus fruits. The gathering was completed by an old maid who knitted sweaters and scarves no one wore. Every time she spoke, she would make a mistake counting her stitches and would have to start all over again while chastising herself out loud: "Shut your mouth, Muteeah."

I abandoned the house, possibly because it was the most depressing of all the houses we lived in. And I divorced my books, too. I stopped reading because I couldn't find any place in that house that was good for reading. I tried to figure out some way to sit that satisfied me or satisfied the image I had of myself reading, but the rooms were dark, and the porch was too narrow for me to stretch my legs, plus it positioned me facing the drab walls and clotheslines hanging at the building across from ours, which was separated from us by a ditch where food scraps and formless junk got tossed.

I abandoned the house during the day, and I abandoned reading altogether, possibly because wandering through Beirut was like a journey into a big fairytale that substituted for the imaginings and mysteries in the stories. And so, I left my books packed in their boxes just as I had carried them with me from the summer village, and I started going to the university on foot. I spent the day on the streets reading everything that could be read: the street names if I could find them on signs that no one took care of anymore, the store signs that gouged my eyes with their multiple languages, ad posters and death notices, restaurant menus and prices pasted on the front doors, the names of the buildings' residents listed at their entrances, and the headlines of newspapers in the kiosks. Things that defied reading also beckoned to me – the vibrant colors adorning certain building facades, the wooden window frames, and the towering walls consumed by trellises and wilted flowers, hiding ancient homes and noble families on the verge of extinction, leading a hushed existence with their timeless and unyielding daily routines. The fishermen with their fishing poles standing for hours on the rocks wearing straw hats to shield their heads from the sun. The lady in the back seat of a car driven by a driver in uniform, her identity and intended destination difficult to discern at dusk. The people coming out from the movie theaters into the daylight after bawling through an Indian romance tearjerker. The handful of men hurriedly carrying a coffin to Bashoura Cemetery as though late for some appointment. The women taking their children to the beach. The man sitting at the sidewalk café on a street teeming with pedestrians, all alone, his hair disheveled in every direction and his eyes staring into space as if he were looking into his soul.

I finished my day completely worn out from my addiction to inventing lives for people I knew nothing about beyond their faces and their names and imagining a past and a story for mysterious places. I slowly climbed the stairs to our house on the fourth floor and fell asleep recalling the day's encounter and getting ready for the next one at the university.

I didn't make it past the first few days in the lecture halls. When the literature professor stated in his opening lecture that high moral purpose is one of the fundamentals of a great literary work, I interrupted him to object, much to the surprise and disbelief of my classmates. He allowed me to speak, so I embarked on a defense of the gratuitous nature of creativity and argued it was content just to elicit emotions. We volleyed supporting evidence and examples, and it appeared that the quotes I cited were convincing or that the students wanted to side with their classmate because they gave me a spontaneous and enthusiastic round of applause. So, I left and never went back, not wanting to embarrass the professor who was getting close to retirement. In modern civilization class a few days later, I corrected some of the teacher's information on Fritz Lang and German expressionist cinema. Apart from the philosophy class every Monday at noon, which delved into personalism, followed by existentialism tracing back to Hegel and Descartes all the way to Socrates, all presented as a magical story on the lips of a good-looking professor the girls scrambled to sit in the front row to listen to as he cleverly improvised from memory. Apart from those two fascinating hours that went by in an instant, I spent all the rest of my time in the cafeteria, to the point that some professors never met me until the oral exam at the end of the school year.

I sat by myself at the campus coffee shop, the one like a fishbowl. I practiced solving giant crossword puzzles while drinking cups of bitter coffee one after another and chain-smoking strong brown French cigarettes, lighting one from the butt of the other, amid the noise and the songs blaring from the jukebox and the ideas being exchanged across the tables. I was joined by people like me who'd come from the south or the north with appearances and thick accents that gave them away. I didn't learn anything new from those types, so I ignored them in favor of getting closer to some young women who smoked marijuana and believed in "free love" between the sexes. I met a young man from the Al-Atrash family whom they called "the Prince," which he didn't object to but rather amplified, going on at length about his relatives' heroic deeds during the Jabal Al-Arab revolt in Syria. And I listened to heated discussions about how best to respond to the defeat of the Arab armies in the 1967 war. The final word on the topic came from two young men who had just come back from military operations against the Israeli army. Beirut's secrets and its possibilities multiplied. A light went off in my head.

I convinced my parents that, thanks to my excellent grades, I'd been awarded an all-expenses-paid one-week trip to the American University in Cairo. They were pleased by the news, and off I went with a couple of my new friends to Amman and then on to the Jordan Valley to join the freedom fighters. Actually, my war didn't last long. The moment we arrived, the trainers seized our IDs with unexpected gruffness and gave us new cards they'd made for everyone with silly nicknames and military ranks recorded on them. I was Lieutenant Abu Jaafar of Nablus. They separated us and subjected us to a long interrogation in a tone that didn't make it seem like we were in the same camp as the ones asking the questions. The officer who was holding my Lebanese ID in his hand wanted to know what the word "Maronite" meant, written in the space for religion. I answered that I'm a Christian. He shook his head over and over again, an indication of his doubts about my motives for joining the armed struggle. He found a solution in the end, which was to offer me what he called "backup operations" in procuring provisions or in administration. I informed him in an agitated tone that for a very long time I'd been looking death in the face, and it never scared me. I had shut the eyes of the slain, dressed corpses in clean shirts, combed their hair. And I added by way of encouraging him that on some occasions I'd stolen their rings and whatever money was in their pockets. That piqued his interest. He asked me to continue, so I plunged into stories about my hometown while he shared the daily happenings in Al-Zarqa Palestinian refugee camp in Jordan, where he'd spent the better part of his youth. He agreed to enlist me in the "Interior Operations" division after he'd caught a glimpse of madness in my eyes that suited the mission I was aspiring to. I quickly trained on confrontation and storming tactics—jumping through a ring of fire, climbing rope, crawling long distances under barbed wire, and shooting at fixed targets and moving targets—until the promised day finally came.

We crossed the Jordan River and set up camp at night. There were three of us—a Palestinian, an Egyptian, and me—behind a small hill that we were told exposed an enemy military route. From there we glimpsed faint lights and heard dogs barking in the distance. In the chilly hours before dawn I felt a stubborn desire for some individuals or an enemy vehicle to appear within our sights so we could shoot at them. The Kalashnikov in my hands seemed to have lost its patience. I would have fired a random shot into the pitch-black night had my two comrades not held me back. We ate cans of food that I think were past their expiration dates, which led to a severe case of diarrhea that repeatedly sent me running into the wild to relieve myself. Day broke and lit up green slopes. It seemed promising but there was no sighting of the enemy, so we went back to where we came from. Another officer who oversaw operations attributed my bout of diarrhea to my supposed fear of confrontation. I denied the accusation and told him to ask my comrades so they could vouch for me, but he returned my ID and dismissed me after thanking me for my sympathies, especially since the number of conscripts asking to join the armed Palestinian cause during that time was much greater than the need. I spent some time adrift in Amman and then went back to Beirut with my tail between my legs.

I had been gone for twenty days. My mother feared I was following in her sister's footsteps, and my paternal aunt silently lamented the notion that she was never going to see me again and was going to die unconsoled. But Sunday at noon I opened the door, raised my arms, and sarcastically shouted in Latin Julius Caesar's famous line, *"Veni, vidi, vici."* I didn't see anything on my trip, but I came and found that my father had been let go from his job. It seems that he'd encouraged the employees to unionize, and when they staged their first strike, the owners of Red Shoe discovered that they were no longer immune to those sorts of demonstrations that were cropping up all over Beirut. Their investigations led them to my father, so they fired him. I came back and found him disgruntled, unwilling to surrender, saying over and over that the war on capitalism was a long one. He'd conclude with a verse from the Gospel: "He who perseveres to the end will be saved."

In his hometown and among friends, my father made a point of introducing himself as a communist. People would be shocked to hear it as he waved a book of Karl Marx quotations in their faces, an Arabic translation he'd partially memorized and would quote from to embellish discussions at his cobbler shop, where he used to meet before the outbreak of bloody events. Unemployed attendees would crowd around him and his artisans. He'd post newspaper clippings for them on the walls, and old adages like "Good deeds sever the tongues" or "The honest merchant is blessed with honest profit, while the hoarder is cursed," and headlining them in bold letters was a verse from the Gospel of Matthew:

"Consider the birds of the sky: They don't sow or reap or gather into barns, yet your heavenly Father feeds them. Aren't you worth more than they?"

My father would go on about the power of labor and its transformation into a commodity and about the exploitation of human beings and cowardly capital, concluding his commentary with the slogan of the ideal city, "From each according to his ability, to each according to his needs." His notion of justice was much like Robin Hood's, and though he said he was a communist, we never knew him to have any party comrades or saw him meet with anyone. He was playing a solo. And he was not an atheist, as if he'd skipped that chapter in socialist literature. He remained devoted to the precepts of the church and was a member of the fraternity of "The Sacred Heart of Jesus." He helped build a huge creche at Christmas time. I saw him on many occasions whispering with the priest and walking in funerals wearing the banner of the fraternity, not embarrassed in the least.

Ready-made shoes made their way to the town early on. One of the craftsmen betrayed his colleagues and opened a shop for men's and women's shoes. The other craftsmen contended that he only did it because he wasn't skilled at making shoes himself and had an easier time selling the prefabricated ones. The demand for women's shoes was very strong because the shoemakers in town made only one simple style for them. Some of the cobblers convened a meeting at our house, which we weren't allowed to attend. The night after, some unknown assailants broke into the ready-made shoe shop. They smashed the windows and scattered the boxes everywhere but didn't steal anything. In the morning, my father was arrested and taken to the police station, where he spent the night with his comrades. They couldn't pin the damages on anyone, but they made all the detainees sign a document vowing to respect competition even though my father remained insistent that that type of competition was not honorable. My father—whose principles I would soon adopt myself even if from behind a thick fog of ideas and big names advocating for the abolition of private property, those anarchists, or scientific socialists as distinguished from the utopian dreamers.

When I returned to the university cafeteria, I avoided talking about my trip to the Jordan Valley. I quit talking altogether. I sat alone, smoking just as compulsively as ever, continuously feeding coins into the jukebox to keep the music resounding through the place. The smell of the sea reached the university, and the colors that managed to survive urbanism in the streets of Beirut—oleander and magnolia flowers—heralded the coming of spring.

One time I spotted in the distance what I thought were the summer twins carrying shopping bags and walking down the sidewalk on Hamra Street where the road starts to slope down toward the amusement park. I hurried after them, but they disappeared around a corner, so I never managed to catch up with them. I realized that all this time since we'd come to Beirut I'd never tried to find their address, even though I knew they lived in the capital.

The seasons came in succession and the city lowered the curtain on its riddles. Just like that, in those streets that clamored with life, I sank back into that depression I'd thought was only inherent to the apparitions of my original hometown and its muddy lanes. I was on the verge of reopening my boxes of books to renourish myself with imaginings and tragic fates when I happened to meet a young man in the last year of his history degree, whose uprightness and way of presenting his ideas appealed to me.

He was one of the few around who didn't smoke, having suffered from asthma since childhood. He'd get away from the smoke and stroll down the sidewalks with anyone who liked to listen to him, so I volunteered for that. I rushed after him. He was Aristotle and I was his walking interlocutor. Sometimes we'd till the seaside corniche up and down or set sail amid the commotion of Souq al-Najjareen: the carpenters' souq, and Souq al-Dhahab: the gold souq. When we'd reach Sharih al-Masarif (Banks Street), the atmosphere would become charged and my friend's voice would grow louder, turning into a sermon against finance capital—that blood sucker with no nation and no morals. He drew the attention of passersby, going on about religion and school and family, calling those things the ideological state apparatus that reproduces class power relations by means of training obedience and acceptance of oppression as it is and the punishing of rebels such as the two of us. He had an intense anger inside him and said that revolution can only be quenched with blood.

He enjoyed my company because, as he put it, I was a skilled conversationalist, even though I only recall myself as someone who mostly listened to him. He took solace in knowing my father was a worker who lived by the power of his own labor. He asked me which neighborhood we lived in. He shook his head and said it was mixed with country folk who were new migrants to the city, mostly from the north, and urbanite laborers or "petite bourgeoisie." The city of Beirut and the details of its history were present in his mind in the form of a war map. All he was missing was a long conductor's baton to point out where the battles were expected to break out and who the various opposing factions were. Always the poor against the rich, war to the death. He talked about his family, too, especially his mother, who raised them "by the sweat of her brow." She worked as a housemaid while his "biological" father, as he called him, neglected them to chase after his whims. And he liked to say, most likely quoting someone, "I was born of a woman and oblivion."

Just when I was beginning to feel like we were rebuilding the world together, my friend asked me at the end of one of those walks to start calling him by his new name: Leon. He wanted to get used to it because he was going to embark on "secret operations." His life was about to change. He was getting some new carefully-forged identification papers. I was completely deflated. He bid me farewell, gave me a big hug, and vanished just as he'd planned, but he wasn't gone from my sight for long. A month later I saw his picture posted on a ficus tree at the entrance to the university. A martyr from an obscure little political party called the Arab Trotskyists Organization. It seemed he was their first fatality, and their last as far as I know.

Gone was my preacher who never quit talking about the long-sought-after earthly paradise, focusing all his efforts on describing how to reach it. That was a path strewn with pain and deprivation. As I walked along the same streets, alone, and ate by myself in cheap restaurants, I could not conquer the grief of losing him.

Then one day when I was going up an escalator in one of the new shopping centers, I spotted one of the twins coming down on the other side. We caught each other's eye and called out to each other in unison. We hugged and sat down in a café to fill each other in about our lives from the day they left the village. I wasn't sure which of the sisters I was talking to. I took a hard look at her features but couldn't ascertain if she was my intimate friend, the one with the fertile imagination and seductive games. I was afraid to make a mistake, so I stuck to generalities—how quickly time flies, how beautiful the village where we met was—and when it came time to leave, I walked a few steps with her before we parted ways. Suddenly, she turned and asked me, smiling shyly, "You don't recognize me, do you?" to which she added when I hesitated, "I'm the sister that you didn't fall for!"

We stood there in front of the expensive perfume shop not knowing what to do with our hands or which way to look. Then in a soft voice I could hardly hear her say, "My sister died. Her husband murdered her."

I felt a light pain in the back of my head.

"He watched her and followed her to her boyfriend's house. She always had a boyfriend. Her life with her husband made her feel terribly lonely, more than if she'd lived alone. He emptied every last bullet from his revolver into them. Her lover was married, too."

I remembered reading something along those lines in a newspaper report that identified the people by their first initials, under the headline, "He snuck up on her and caught her by surprise. Two bodies, one suspect." And it said the killer turned himself in to the police voluntarily. She grabbed a tissue and wiped the tears from her eyes. We went out onto a balcony overlooking the city and a question flashed in my mind:

"Was she married when I met you there?" I asked, pointing in the direction of the mountains.

"Yes. Her husband worked in Kuwait, and we would spend the summer in the nicer climate here. I tried to get close to you to prevent her from getting into trouble all over again, but what could I do? Men like her. You weren't an exception to the rule. She had a special magnetism."

She burst into tears. Before saying goodbye, she told me she had kept something for me. A bundle of letters her sister had asked her to keep so they wouldn't fall into the hands of her husband, who was always searching through her things.

"She would come visit me from time to time to reread the letters. She said that your writings gave her the strength to go on. She always left my place with her spirits lifted."

We agreed to meet again. It was a silent meeting. She handed me the letters.

"I read some of them while my sister was still alive. Writings with a strong pulse that I could feel but didn't understand very much."

The sister gave me her phone number. I didn't ask her any questions I might regret hearing the answers to. I wanted her to stay the way I had known her during a summer after which I lost my language. A season that went by in the blink of an eye, like a flash of lightning in a friendly night sky. As for the letters, I stuffed them into one of my boxes of books without opening them.

I called the sister again two weeks later. It rang but I couldn't stay on the line. The next time, she answered. I heard her voice, hesitated, and hung up. Finally, after a game of cat and mouse, I said hello. She said she was happy to hear from me, and we made plans to get together. She told me that her sister's husband was going to take advantage of the extenuating circumstances provisions of the honor crime law, especially since his crime had been committed in broad daylight—in flagrante delicto. At any rate, he didn't have much prison time left.

After offering condolences and reminiscing over that summer, we easily made our way to the bedroom. But at the first kiss, a chill descended on us that took away all our desire. The two of us imagined, at the same moment, the deceased sister with her short haircut lying there between us on the bed. We jumped up, fleeing that image, and put on our clothes.

"It's like reheated leftovers," I said to her, and we parted without saying goodbye. I ran into her again by chance in Martyrs' Square. When I spotted her in the distance walking past Cinema Rivoli, I quickly ducked out of sight. She might have seen me too and hurried on her way as well.

As for gaining victory for my betrayed friend, I concealed a screwdriver in my jacket and went around scratching luxury cars at night—Jaguars and Mercedes—or slashed their tires in abandoned alleys. One night, I found myself in front of the window of a bank, so I threw a rock, breaking the glass, and ran away. I looked for comrades of his, other members of that organization, but didn't have any luck. It was said that they were extremely secretive and that the total number of members could be counted on one's fingers. I read their books that pulled the curtain off the world, in sharp contrast with the ones that had kept me company up until that point, which cast the shadow of myth over the world. As an appetizer, I devoured *Permanent Revolution*, *The Prophet Armed* and an abridged version of *Das Kapital*. Then I dove into dialectical materialism and the alienation of laborers from their true interests. I put on my departed friend's accent and his excited manner of presenting his opinions, and I lured a young woman into accompanying me on my wanderings through the streets. In fact, I had become skilled at attracting young women with my stock of literary and poetic wares that intoxicated them. She would look at me intensely, ask me about my friends and my theory of women, and I would answer her about the workings of the economic apparatus and the possibilities of the city right there before our eyes. Her enthusiasm cooled, and she quit accompanying me.

Three years after we descended from the high mountains to the university where I managed to get a literature degree while exerting the least bit of effort possible I dedicated only one week to reviewing lessons each semester—I felt I'd warmed up to the city. It no longer smacked me with its illusions that throbbed from over-exploration and its names whose identity I was constantly trying to guess, to the point that I ventured a prediction of the kinds of momentous events it would witness, guided by what I had seen and read and what my departed friend had supplied me with. I'd stretch my legs at the café with complete confidence and start preaching to the influx of new freshmen arriving in the city that capitalism produces its own crisis. I developed a moral authority, quoting numbers for the distribution of wealth in the country and the fifty families that enjoyed the largest share while leaving crumbs for all the rest. As a gesture of loyalty to my deceased friend, I would declare, using the same rhetorical phrasing he tied his thoughts together with, that this disgraceful disparity guaranteed that in the near future the social strife would explode and wipe out the system of the ruling party along with it. And this, of course, is what did not happen. Rather, some other genie popped out of the city's bottle.

EPIPHÄNOMEN

MY AUNT DIED. A case of "sudden death," which doesn't usually strike women. She'd told me once in a hushed voice that she caught yellow fever during a trip to the city of Manaus in the Amazon with her husband, Fernando. She spent a whole week lying all alone under a mosquito net, nursed by a young girl who was afraid of being infected herself, while Fernando went chasing after black women. She recovered but never stopped worrying about a relapse. She expected the "*vomito negro*" virus to pop out of her suitcase, but instead she got hit with a heart attack that took her down in a matter of minutes.

We laid her out on her bed in her prettiest dress. I didn't weep for her. I sat on a chair beside her, not taking my eyes off her face, contemplating her pallor, and imagining that in her silence she was recalling the story of her life that she had entrusted to me. It was hard for me to believe that the dead just faded away. I took advantage of no one being around for a moment to take out a cosmetic pad from her makeup case. I dipped it in pink powder and rubbed it on her cheeks just like I used to see her do every day. And I put her expensive pearl necklace around her neck and watched carefully until they closed the coffin, making sure no one snatched it off her.

My father refused to take her all the way to our hometown. He paid some money to have her buried in the nearly forsaken Syriac cemetery in Beirut. We sat in the reception room of a nearby church and received condolences. It was the dead of winter. Over the course of the day, eighteen people came in. I had fun counting them. They included the priest, his assistant, and some unemployed folks who swarm to a death even if they have no connection whatsoever to the deceased. Half of them attended the funeral service. The church was cold, and the priest rushed through his litanies as if there were a fire under his butt, and that was that.

My beautiful aunt was gone. She was like a crystal vase in our house with a bouquet of peonies in it. Her room remained locked up just as it was. Our house became all the more melancholy, and my mother all the lonelier. My father found a new job after being let go from Red Shoe and went back to his old habit of staying out of the house all day. Our Armenian neighbor also left for Burj Hammoud at the eastern edge of the city. I was there the day she said goodbye to us. All she said was, "This area isn't for us. You better watch out."

She was anticipating events to come, but we didn't give much weight to her words. Elephantiasis disabled our Beiruti neighbor with the loud voice and appetizing recipes. The apartment lost all its flavor, so we too decided to move once again, but we headed west.

My aunt's death sent me back to our hometown for the first time since having been forced to leave it. My father asked me to go with him during a truce of sorts that had prevailed there. We went to the government palace to obtain a copy of my aunt's death certificate so I could transfer her bank account to my name, as she had specified in her will. And we also wanted to get a new identity card for me because I'd lost my old one, or so I claimed. The Civil Status registrar looked at me with surprise and said to my father, an old acquaintance of his, "He's all grown up. He's a man now."

I quarreled with the clerk with the beautiful handwriting because he hastened to fill in the place on my new ID for religion without asking me first, while on the other hand he'd left the spaces for level of education, occupation, eye color, skin color, and the shape of my nose all blank. The registrar addressed my father again, ignoring my complaint.

"It seems he's a communist just like you."

My father grinned.

We no longer had a home or any relatives in the town. My father was an only child now that his sister had died, and my mother's sister had flown off to Ivory Coast.

We waited around for an hour or so. There weren't any traces of the fighting left except black dresses and headscarves worn by women who appeared and disappeared in the alleyways. I recalled the smell of places. I knew them by heart. Now that we had left this place, I suddenly wished I could sit on a wicker chair in front of the little stone doorstep across from the church and listen to the sounds of the town while watching the passersby until nightfall.

On our way back to Beirut, I secretly sneered about the registrar's surprise over me. I was "a man now," he said. My profile was complete. I'd obtained a bachelor of arts degree without exerting any special effort. Like a camel of the desert, I'd stored up a lot of knowledge in my hump from my years of schooling and reading. For the literature essays on exams, I would resort to suggesting to the examiner that I knew more about the given topic than I'd disclosed. This ploy worked every time.

My aunt left me all her money plus the interest. The money from her husbands and lovers and the Colombian lottery winnings—a million pesos at the time, which she had kept secret from everyone but me. I grew a mustache and went out with women from time to time—fleeting relationships that amounted to nothing more than aroused bodies and shallow souls.

I came across the twin sister again on a crowded public bus. We exchanged greetings from afar. The girl seemed to have lost her youthfulness somehow. She looked baffled. A red rose that only blooms in resonance with her sister. Maybe I had become a man as my father's friend said, but the lone wolf inside me wasn't visible to the eye.

We migrated west inside the capital to a house I chose because my father was busy working his new job six days a week. He would take his time sprucing himself up every morning, then he'd pay for the two seats in the front of the taxi beside the driver and head off to work, not returning until evening. On Sundays, he'd take my mother on a little outing to Raouche. They'd sit in one of the cafés drinking orange juice and watching the sunset while my mother secretly hoped to see one of those desperados who'd reached the end of his rope and decided to throw himself off the towering rock.

I chose our next house, in my new role as the rich one in the family. A one-story house with a small staircase leading up to it from Makhoul Street, a little yard wrapping around it with loquat and fig trees and cactus plants. It had high frescoed ceilings and was welcoming, bright, and had been designed with precision and care. It was classified as a historic building, which doubled the rent—the kind of house you might imagine still retains the voices and ghosts of the people who have lived in it through the years. The previous family took all its contents with them except for an expensive Yamaha piano they decided not to haul away the day they brought a moving truck for their furniture. The owner of the house didn't have much praise for his house's architecture and seemed not to care about promoting its uniqueness amid all the multi-story concrete buildings surrounding it. He told me that the previous occupants didn't want to take the piano with them because it reminded them of their young son, the one who played it, who had been killed along with his new bride in a car accident one week after their wedding. They moved to some other place for the same reasons that prompted our Armenian neighbor to move. There was something going on in the city that the papers didn't write about, and that people didn't circulate out loud, and which my father and I didn't want to take into consideration as we tried to get our lives in order.

To the piano I added a Tinawi painting. I had left the walls of the main hall empty for months until I could plan a trip to one of those poor Damascus neighborhoods. I was convinced that folk art was beautiful precisely because it was of the people. I went to the studio whose owner had died, and without much haggling came back with a painting of Antara. He was on the back of a horse, with Abla behind him. The horse had a big black tail much like the knight's moustache. The tail didn't fit within the space of the canvas, so the artist added the missing part of it to the top of the painting. He was "conscientious" and didn't cheat his customers, as the seller and inheritor of his paintings said, adding that he didn't know how to read or write. I hung the painting, which was adorned with a thousand colors plus two lines from the famous Mu'allaqa of Antara, in the salon where the piano still stood, its hefty presence taking up a good portion of the room. That was when, just as my vision for our new house was taking shape—including a special room for my aunt's belongings that we kept locked up—we heard the first sounds of gunfire in the Beirut sky. We didn't pay much attention, my father and I, to what was happening around us because we were absorbed in other matters far removed from the goings on that we were attending to on the surface. Each of us had his own hidden agenda. Two double lives.

My father was in love, and at his age falling in love comes on strong. He had no idea that the war that had started sputtering around us was a kind of aphrodisiac. He'd reached his mid-fifties, having married young, and now found himself compensating in one go for his years of devotion to a woman who gave little attention to her femininity. He managed his Beirut love affair with absolute secrecy and with the careful attention to detail of a patient, skilled artisan until one day when the phone gave him away.

That old black Ericsson phone that rang like a bell, waking everyone up. My father's lover was missing him at night while he lay beside my mother, so she called the house. Most likely he had asked her to avoid risking a scandal, but as soon as darkness fell her desire for him would flare up and she would do anything to hear his voice. The phone would ring, and my mother would try to wake him up while he evaded answering by pretending to be deep asleep. My mother would go out to the parlor, but the moment she'd pick up the phone the caller would hang up. One evening when I had come home early, I discovered how similar my voice was to my father's when I reached the phone before my mother. I heard the heavy sighs of a woman calling me by my father's name and thought she had dialed the wrong number. She finished her rebuke for leaving her all alone with that "jackass," by whom I supposed she meant her husband. It appeared that my father had lost control of her, so he resorted to unplugging the phone before bed, which I discovered because one time he forgot to plug it back in in the morning.

After graduating from the university, I started teaching at Ibn Khaldun high school, a public school for boys. The students were sons of small grocery store owners or internal security conscripts, who were of limited income or poor. I'd arrive in the chilly mornings to stand before a bunch of adolescents who knew nothing of the French language except a few scattered expressions, now that the successive violent incidences had begun and had brought with them some ready-made slogans like fighting colonialism and resisting the smear campaign against the nation, giving those students the upper hand in the balance of power between them and Racine and La Fontaine. Explaining a scene from a play in which Orestes expresses his impossible love was an occasion to prove that my mission was also virtually impossible. They would never understand the language, and the tragedy of the Greek hero cursed by the gods wasn't ever going to reach them at any level. Their poor vocabulary and simplistic usage in that language of the enemy made them sound like babies when they spoke it. Subject, verb, object, in the best-case scenario.

I made a point from day one not to speak to them except in French, which led them to think that I didn't know any other language or that I was a stranger to their country. My light-colored eyes and fair complexion aided in that belief. But one day I blew up in response to a student's blockheadedness as he acted like a smartass while reading La Fontaine's fable, "Donkey loaded with sponges, Donkey loaded with salt." I got off my teacher's chair and shouted at him in French that he clearly resembled the donkey loaded with sponges. I concluded by quoting the saying, speaking in flawless Arabic.

> Every ailment has a medicine that cures it,
> except for stupidity, which wears out the person
> who tries to fix it.

His buddies couldn't believe their ears. They gave me a jubilant round of applause and we all made up.

That was my overt occupation, for sixteen hours a week, a work shift that allowed me to devote myself to the thing I was even more dedicated to after transforming our house into a headquarters for Arab Trotskyists meetings. Its entire membership attended—five men and two women. My friend the walker who hadn't been fated to survive had given them my name along with high praise for my revolutionary talents, which I never knew I had, unless he meant my lack of caution in the face of challenges and my volunteering for difficult tasks. They had observed my conduct carefully. They inquired about me, held interviews with me, and we decided to hold party meetings at our place.

"Your house doesn't arouse suspicion," they said without elaborating.

They didn't enter the house all together the first time, for security purposes. They cast strange glances at the big Tinawi painting in the entryway and then we got down to business and began a serious discussion in my room about how to confront the life that the capitalist elite created for us without consulting us.

At one point, the fine china vase where my mother always placed any flowers that came her way disappeared from its spot on a table in the parlor. My father couldn't find anyone to blame except the Arab Trotskyists. He called them "those friends of yours who stay awake at night and sleep during the day." He did the same when my mother went looking in her closet for a black fur coat of hers that she rarely wore—she wanted to wear it to church one cold Sunday—but didn't find it. I immediately defended my friends saying they had the highest moral character. The moment my mother started wondering who the thief might be, I knew my hunch was right; it was my father. He had been trying to distance himself from blame by accusing my comrades. He'd given the fur coat to his girlfriend as a gift.

The city was rocking beneath falling bombs and armed attacks. My comrades and I were like a handful of rebels huddling beneath one umbrella against the rain, believing that the sky was clear. We didn't give any particular importance to what was happening around us. We looked at it like a transient event separate from the natural process of the social conflict that we believed would inevitably occur.

"It's a transitory phenomenon," one of the comrades pointed out once, "an epiphänomen," referring to the internecine clashes that felled their victims daily. The poor—on both sides—were the fuel for that war. The killers and the killed. While making his case about the main contradiction and the secondary contradictions, the comrade repeated the term "epiphänomen," which, he supposed, when pronounced properly in its original German would make us feel confident about the validity of our revolutionary choices and their durability. We had our special enemies and our special weapons, which I hid in our house. Three Kalashnikov machine guns, two Belgian handguns, two boxes of French XF1 hand grenades, and numerous sticks of dynamite whose country of origin I was unable to determine. It was the internationalization of weapons in preparation for launching the internationalization of the struggle that was dear to the heart of our inspirer, who got stabbed in the back with an ice pick in Mexico. We brought the weapons into the house near dawn when my parents were fast asleep and put them under the bed in my aunt's room, where I had arranged all her things exactly the way she'd set them up herself: her mirror in the heart-shaped frame on top of the table and her makeup kit ready for use and her thick white embroidered pillows stacked up on her

bed, since she slept nearly sitting up after arriving at that
position during a semipermanent state of insomnia. I kept
the key to that room with me at all times, and during our
nightly meetings as well. Our quasi-military group was not
inclined to dwell on intellectual or controversial matters.
What brought its various elements together was the desire
for direct action, that is, missions that begin with the
writing of slogans on the back wall of the Ministry of the
Interior—"Repression will only make us more determined,"
then onto the destruction of the books of Adam Smith and
David Ricardo wherever we found them, in public libraries
or bookstores, finally arriving at the distribution of food-
stuffs to the poor people of the Nabaa neighborhood and
the incitement of women to rise against their husbands and
teaching them to read and write. But our main project that
we spoke about in whispers revolved around vengeance for
our comrade, the namesake of our group.

After long debates about the choice of the target and
the means, we finally did it. Over the course of many days,
one of the women comrades surveilled the man's comings
and goings from his house, and another comrade prepared
a stack of dynamite with a timer. I put on some tennis shoes
and snuck into the garage at night to place the dynamite
under the Jaguar. Then we waited, each one at his own
house. The bank manager's driver was badly bruised by the
explosion that went off when he was parking the car after
the owner had gotten out. The driver was released from the
hospital the same day. The Jaguar was no longer drivable.
And that was the sole bit of damage that was acknowl-
edged in the ensuing condemnations. The man had close
ties to the people of influence. He was a big shot donor to

Dar al-Aytam Orphanage and the vice president of the Beirut Families Union, and he had no enemies. We also found out that he was an old bachelor. "He married the bank," people said. And so, blame was placed on the other side of the city: "They are trying to weaken the nationalists by hitting their vital activities."

On our end, we refrained from claiming responsibility for the act. We were not skilled at timing or making explosives, so our strike ended up being more like stabbing water with a sword.

After that, the "Arab Trotskyists" carried out other operations. I could not fathom from what source of inner energy or what tragedy in their childhoods they drew the power to remain steadfast to the end. They helped some women get abortions, they opened a restaurant where customers could eat their fill while paying whatever amount they could afford, and they also spied on my father with great success.

I asked for their help, and when they found out the reason, some of them objected, since they didn't really condemn infidelity due to their opposition to the institution of marriage altogether. Despite that, two of them agreed to help me, as friends rather than comrades. My father didn't know them, since the meetings at our house were always held after midnight. They got into the same taxi that my father was in, seated by himself up front. They told me that the whole way he kept asking the driver about his income and how many children he had, pushing him to join the revolution, and that his voice sounded so much like mine they were astonished. They almost burst out laughing when they first heard him speak. They monitored him an entire day, from the time he left the shoe factory. They sat at the next table over from him at the restaurant where he had planned to meet up with his girlfriend. A tall blonde, possibly pretty, but it was difficult for them to determine with her face hidden behind dark glasses. They heard her asking him about the pearl necklace he'd been promising her for months. She accused him of lying to her, said he was taking advantage of her, and she also complained about her husband's ways and how stingy he was, especially concerning anything to do with the household. She claimed that all men were the same, all selfish. The two comrades concluded that my father was not having a passionate affair; he was clearly being extorted. One of them added that the ease with which my father was able to meet her in a public place without her showing any signs of discomfort made him think that the blonde's husband was in on his wife's activities or maybe was even encouraging her.

Before confronting my father with the facts, I looked for the pearl necklace in my aunt's room but didn't find it. I remembered that I had kept my eye on her coffin until it was carried from the church to the cemetery, in case anyone tried to open it, but I didn't go to the cemetery with them. I decided to go see the Syriac priest in our former neighborhood. I'd been told that he left and only came on Sundays to say Mass to a small group of parishioners, mostly elderly. He told me at the door of the church where I had been waiting for him that my father, who'd accompanied the gravediggers and the priest to the cemetery, had asked for them to open the coffin so he could take one last look at his sister. "We noticed the necklace. We were surprised," the priest said. "We thought you must have forgotten to remove it from her neck."

Every day my father and I would leave for the city and my mother would sit by herself in the parlor. She'd read a little from the biography of Patriarch Jeremias al-Amshitti and the novel *Shajarat al-Durr* (*Tree of Pearls*) by Jurji Zaydan. She would have started muttering prayers with the prayer beads in her hand, a rosary my aunt had given her as a gift the day she moved in with us. My aunt said she got it from Christ the King Church in Rio de Janeiro. My mother always kept it under her pillow. I sat with her one of the mornings. She made me black coffee and allowed me to smoke while I drank it as she poured out her soul to me. She made up for her long silence in that house where she'd found no neighbors to befriend. All the women in the quarter were educated and haughty. She couldn't find a way to talk to them, so she spent the day all alone.

She burst into tears out of the blue and said her life was bleak. She didn't love us anymore and she no longer had any desire to cook for us. She was speaking in the plural, about the two of us, my father and me, even though it was clear from her words that she was talking only about her husband. She'd known everything about him from the start. The phone calls at night, the long absences that went beyond his daily work shift, and his attention to hygiene and changing his shirt and underwear every morning, in addition to female aromas that he came home with on his clothes after every absence. One morning, she sensed he was getting up earlier than usual, at the crack of dawn. She saw him sneak out with the fine crystal vase and run off with it like a thief. She kept quiet about it because if she exposed his infidelity, she would have to leave the house and she didn't have any place to go. I promised her I would

78

talk to him. I asked my comrades for one last favor, which was difficult for me to justify because it went against their principles, and fortunately, our friendship won out.

My two comrades waited for my father to exit the shoe factory and pulled a gun on him, which they were careful to unload beforehand. They thrust it at his belly and ordered him to get into their car. They drove him to an isolated place by the seashore and started accusing him of being a spy, saying that he was giving the enemy the coordinates of sensitive locations so they could aim their cannons at them. My father vehemently denied it and asked them who this enemy was while the two of them winked at each other and tried not to laugh. They wanted to laugh partly because of his befuddlement and partly because of his voice, which reminded them of me. In the end, they told him to get out of there and go back to his own area where he belonged or else he would get hurt—him and his family too. They added that they knew his only son well, the blond guy who taught French at Ibn Khaldun High School, and they could get to him if he didn't obey their orders. They gave him two weeks to move out. He replied that he didn't know the east side and didn't know anyone there; he came from a town up north. "Forewarned is forearmed," they said before letting him go.

He fell for the ploy. He went home and kept quiet, not sharing his "secret" with a soul, though his behavior started to change. He came home early from work, coddled my mother, and looked at me with suspicion. Less than a week later, someone came along who would make the decision for him and for all of us. One night around dawn we were awakened by a hard knock at the door—the neighbors in their pajamas warning us there was a fire in the northern bedroom of our house—my aunt's bedroom. I got my parents out to the street and went back inside to the burning bedroom. When I opened the door, I unknowingly created an air current that doubled the fire's momentum. I retreated to the parlor. I took down the painting of Antar and Abla and dragged a box of my books and got out of the house. I leaned the Tinawi painting against a tree on the sidewalk, catching the attention of the crowd of people drawn there by the fire, so I could go back and get the other box of books. I shouted at the onlookers in front of the house many times to get out of the way because I was worried the fire would reach the weapons under my aunt's bed. And that's exactly what happened. After a little while, one could hear hand grenades and sticks of dynamite exploding. Fire and smoke billowed up into the air, terrifying the neighborhood. There was a big hole in the outer wall of the house, and the street was crowded with people.

My parents stayed in a nearby hotel while I took refuge at the house of one of the resistance comrades. The next morning, I accompanied my father to the police station where we were told it was arson. They asked us if we suspected anyone, so my father told them how he'd been abducted and threatened. The policemen were smoking cigarettes and recording complaints in the big register book, the only thing they could do because they were incapable of enforcing anything or punishing anyone. But upon our return to inspect what was left of our things, we met an architect from the historical home preservation society who'd come to assess the damages. He said he was sure there was someone who wanted to destroy the old historical home in order to put up a multi-story building in its place,a small skyscraper that would stream a lot of money to the owners of the land and the house. That was what was happening all over the capital in recent times. The landlord came too. He didn't seem bereaved in the least. In fact, I can say with confidence that he was pleased with what happened. My father on the other hand was convinced that the two men who'd threatened him at the seashore were the ones who'd set the house on fire. But when he recalled the scene, he couldn't believe that those young men were capable of harm. He felt he knew them, that he'd seen them before. He looked at me a long time as though he was coming close to solving the puzzle.

"They know you," he said. "And they know where you teach."

I was scared we would be caught, so I let him believe what he wanted. He felt even more strongly that we were living in a hostile environment and started saying that we had left our hometown to escape the very thing we ended up finding in the capital.

My aunt's room was completely charred. A section of the house collapsed. It was no longer inhabitable. We had no other choice but to move away. The "epiphenomenon" that we had taken lightly had chased us down and forced us into a new migration. Every material trace of my aunt vanished. I only managed to find a few of her things. Fire had eaten up everything she'd saved as evidence of her travels and romances. There was nothing left except the pearl necklace that I imagined the tall blonde, my father's lover, flaunted if ever she was invited to a wedding or a circumcision celebration. That was also my aunt's final death.

MY FRIENDLY GHOSTS

THEY WELCOMED US as though we were survivors of certain doom. They shook our hands, squeezing them hard, and welcomed us back "among family." An elderly man who introduced himself as the mayor of the district, two young volunteers, and some women who lived nearby came to see us. We had no idea where they emerged from the moment we arrived. I was about to correct them and say that we were not really returning because we'd never lived there a single day. We were newcomers getting lost in their streets, which I discovered coiled around each other like a maze, like the game of snakes and ladders. But I didn't want to spoil their fun.

They secretly chuckled at our heavy accent while we snickered at the way they mixed random French words in with everything they said in Arabic. They were convinced, without a shred of evidence, that the people who'd set our house on fire while we slept inside over on the other side of the capital wanted to kill us, wanted to force us out. And as a result, one of them added, we were their prize in the open war between the two Beiruts. They brought us food and offered us clothing. They came inside and helped us set up the furniture in an apartment whose previous tenants, we later discovered, had moved out to escape the war—but in the opposite direction. They scrutinized the pieces of furniture that we'd been able to fit in one truck in our move. They stood in wonder in front of the painting of Antar and Abla, while one of the two young men tripped over his words as he read aloud the two lines of poetry that had been drawn in calligraphy to embellish the horse's saddle.

> I bestowed upon him a quick stab
> With the straight and solid sword in my hand
> Then I thrusted my mute lance into his armor
> For there are no rules against piercing a noble man

The man misread every word of the famous *mu'allaqa*. He didn't understand the meaning of the poetry, but he'd caught a whiff of the boasting in it. He stated that the only thing Arabs have ever been any good at since the day God created them was fake heroism. Our hosts were relieved by our names, which were those of saints and early martyrs of the church. They were fond of our family name as well—my father's family, which was known for its learned and devout men of religion who lived in past centuries, one of whom was a monk who would wash his habit and then fling it into the sun's rays to dry. Their overwhelming concern for us didn't match the looks on our faces. Only my mother showed any semblance of satisfaction about what our circumstances had led us to. She smiled at them politely and thanked them for their help. My father, with that scowl on his face, looked like someone condemned to hard labor. He exaggerated losing work on the other side of the city, claiming that it would be difficult at his advanced age to find anyone to employ him here. As for me, my plan was to accompany my folks to their new residence, get them settled in, and hurry back to my school and comrades. Our heroic missions weren't finished yet, weren't ever going to be finished. Our fighting spirit was still strong.

I tried to go back a few days later. The taxi driver dropped me off at the national museum and said I just had to walk a short distance down Abdallah al-Yafi Boulevard which was packed with obstacles and embankments. Dozens of people, their faces tired, were trying to cross the demarcation line, dragging along their children and their suitcases. Most of them were headed to the airport on the other side. They were emigrating, leaving a city that had become difficult to live in. The avenue was closed off at the end—with concrete blocks on both sides, leaving between them a single lane for pedestrians, with a piece of wood with writing on it that said, "Crossing open from 8 AM to 4 PM" just like school hours or government office hours. It was guarded by armed men who asked for IDs and asked crossing pedestrians where they were going and why they were crossing. Each of us had a story, and the armed men were not in a hurry. I listened intermittently to a couple in front of me in line. They mentioned their sick son, and said they were coming back from visiting him in the hospital for pulmonary diseases. The wife burst out crying and the armed men comforted her. My turn came. It seems they were following an alternating system of being sympathetic one time and being hostile the next. It was my luck to get frowning faces and gruff questions. They scrutinized my ID and grimaced even more.

"Where to?" one of them asked crossly.

"Makhoul Street."

They didn't like my terse answer, or they thought I was mocking them, because they had never heard of Makhoul Street before. If only my friend the walker had been with me, he would have known everything about who they were and where they were from by their clothes and their accents. He might have established that they belonged to what he called the lumpen proletariat, incidental newcomers to the city who were happy about its destruction because it was their only means to obtaining some sort of spoils from it.

They gave back my ID and ordered me to go back to where I came from. That was my opportunity. I explained to them that my house was over there, and I had a valuable piano that I wanted to retrieve. I told them I was going to put flowers on my aunt's grave. How could I abandon her there in the Syriac cemetery on the other side of the capital? My pleading tone didn't help me. Pointing toward the east, they barked their orders: *Your place is there. Go back.*

They'd read it on my ID card, assumed it from my name and its clear sectarian origins. They raised their voices, not understanding how their orders could be disobeyed, but I ignored their demand and proceeded towards the crossing. Deep inside me was a constant craving for confrontation. I never protect my back when I attack. Two of them stood in my way, so I pushed them, armed only with my right to pass. One of them raised his machine gun and cocked it. I didn't budge from my place one iota. I finished up by saying, while looking at my wristwatch, that my freshmen high school students, literature section, were expecting me at Ibn Khaldun High School. They got fed up with me and my details that didn't mean a thing to them and my mention of strange places they'd never heard of. After his warning me and my refusing to obey his demand, one of them fired at the ground. Shrapnel flew up from several shots, one of which hit me in the leg. The people waiting at the crossing fled in every direction. Some militia men bound my leg while cursing me. I held myself together, not feeling any pain despite the gush of blood. An ambulance arrived and took me back to where I'd come from. On the way to the hospital, the pain hit me. I stifled my moaning before they gave me an injection of sedatives. They put my leg in a cast.

"It should stay in the cast for forty days," the doctor said. At home I raised it up on the bed where I lay, and where my mother came to tell me that she'd resigned herself to praying for me to just stay alive because getting close to danger flowed in my veins. My father wanted to know what happened to me in detail. He wanted me to describe the crossing point and reiterate to him the questions the armed men had asked me. I suspected that he was scouting the situation in order to attempt to make the crossing himself, over to where his heart was still calling him.

I'd been locked out. The Beirut that my leftist friend had sketched for me—that city bustling with throngs of country folk rushing to it and to the cleanliness of its deep-rooted bourgeois places—had vanished. The small tradesmen over here, the Armenians with their industrial skills over there, the seaside with its hotels, the belles and the spies, the Ottoman souqs, the street of sidewalk cafés, the cinema houses, the educated elites, the quiet residential neighborhood more like a village smack in the middle of Beirut where my father and mother and I lived. We lived there after leaving the west side, because my friend's tumultuous city had been reduced to just two camps: the Muslim one and the Christian one. It was fortunate that he died without seeing that happen.

I removed the cast from my leg and got out of bed. I discovered I was unable to step forward without leaning to the right side, so the doctor recommended the use of a cane. I was turned off by the idea, but he reassured me that I would need it for no more than two or three months. I went out onto the sidewalk with it and walked carefully, measuring my steps. I liked seeing my reflection in the store windows—a fleeting ghost that awakened in me some literary memories. The cane gave me some stability and control. And I had no fear of it affecting my standing with women. On the contrary, I was confident that having it would only make me more obscure and more attractive. Rather than working towards ridding myself of it by practicing walking on my own, I acquired a collection of canes—ten or so, made of walnut wood or elder. I even found a gold knob shaped like a cat head at an antique shop. The seller sold it to me at double the price as soon as I showed my enthusiasm. After several months during which I regained my health while my bones healed and straightened, I refused to let go of the cane. I continued to lean on it as I walked even though I didn't need it. I'd rush down the stairs, and then when I went out to the street to mix in with the pedestrians I'd go back to my sluggish gait and turn into a stylish cultured man, a dandy who'd made appearances into a reason for living.

The cane and my new alienation brought me back to my books, the ones that I had abandoned while searching for revolutionary truth in writings that are not content with anything less than world history and humankind as a topic. I opened my boxes. I rediscovered my books, on benches and at desks, in my bedroom and in the bathroom. I bought more of them. I would read and not finish what I'd started, embarking on paths I promised myself to resume traversing at a later time. I couldn't finish a book anymore. I was sure that I couldn't bear endings. All final pages were sad. And every time I dropped into a movie theater since we'd left Beirut, I'd stand up and leave before the end of the film the moment it appeared to me that the events unfolding on the screen were nearing a conclusion. I was most comfortable with books that had no beginning and no end. I could open to any page and it would be readable and comprehensible, stories that advanced without a clear trajectory. That was how I finished the Old Testament—moving randomly from Lot's wife to Noah's flood and then on to the rebuilding of the temple—in excerpts out of sequence.

Books were my only companions on this side of the city that we'd settled down in in a three-bedroom apartment—one for my parents, one for me to sleep in with my retrieved books and dreams, and one kept locked up in my aunt's name where we put some of her shoes that survived the fire. The very next day after we arrived, and perhaps due to our apathetic reaction or because they'd heard some disconcerting political talk about us, such as that we had an affiliation for the other side (the same one that had kicked us out), the neighbors stopped visiting us and left us to fend for ourselves.

Our life didn't get any better. We continued to feel my father's anxiety and ensuing endeavors to get back to the scene of his marital betrayal. We didn't know if he succeeded in crossing to the other side, but he was gone for a whole day and didn't come back until morning. His mood stayed mercurial. Some days he joked around with us, but my mother didn't even crack a smile. That was followed by bouts of depression when he wouldn't join us for lunch. We read him like an open book, my mother and I.

My mother ... oh my dear mother. Once she surpassed age fifty, my mother remembered herself. She woke up to the anguish she'd been concealing inside herself. That happened with no warning. I came home from school at noon the day after Palm Sunday to have lunch with my parents. I'd started working at the nearby Good Shepherd High School. I tapped the door with my cane to announce my arrival, but my mother was nowhere to be found. She usually never left the house. The food was on the table, cold. Lunch for two only. Peas with meat and rice, beet salad, and julep juice with pine nuts and raisins. She hadn't factored in a setting for herself. She wasn't coming back.

When my father came home, a look of fear washed over his eyes. We had no idea where to look for my mother in the city, so we sat there in silence until a knock came at the door. She came in with a woman who'd come along with the crowd of people that welcomed us the first day of our forced migration from the west side. The woman was smiling, flustered, and my mother was wearing clothes that she'd put on for the first time: a soft blue velvet dress and the only hat she owned—the one with a feather on top that she had been wearing in her wedding pictures.

She'd hidden it inside a drawer and forgotten about it. She had kohl eyeliner on, just as my aunt always told her she should do, adding that she was beautiful, while my mother shrugged off the compliment. She looked funny. My eyes welled up, so I went closer to the window to watch the action out on the street, hoping she wouldn't see me. She tossed the hat onto the sofa and sat down dejected, her eyes wandering. Then she asked us why we didn't eat our lunch, and we didn't know how to answer.

The woman started to leave, so I followed her to the building entrance, forgetting my cane in my excitement. She told me that she had seen my mother sitting at Jesuits Park, laughing to herself and looking lost. She approached her, but my mother didn't recognize her, possibly because they'd only met once before. She sat down beside her on the bench, and my mother spoke of how her family had suffered from hunger during the Great War. Her grandfather would sell an olive tree in exchange for two or three loaves of bread, enough food to feed his children for one day. She'd had an arranged marriage and wanted no more children; her only son—me, I guess—had been conceived by accident.

She said her family was not fit to have children. She didn't say why, and the woman was embarrassed to ask. When the woman got up to leave the garden, my mother asked for help getting back home. Lots of people get lost along those similar-looking streets. She accompanied her to the vicinity of the house, but my mother stood there looking confused and not recognizing the place, so she led her to the apartment. I thanked the woman and went back to find that my mother had changed her clothes, put away her hat, and washed her face. I jested with her and cracked jokes while we ate lunch, and we turned the page as if nothing had happened. We never mentioned it again after that.

We resumed our life. My father found work, but he wasn't happy. He managed a shop that sold expensive imported shoes. He didn't like the work shift. My condition stabilized once again. Teaching wasn't difficult. The students at The Good Shepherd were more familiar with the French language. And so, my days fell into a pattern on the fringe of things. A little teacher, third tier, tax ID 67-280, eligible for a promotion every two years, admired by his colleagues who didn't think twice about asking for his help if they were faced with any sort of language-related problem. The teachers whose looks and personalities I had no interest in tried to cozy up to me, while the philosophy teacher in the senior classes—who was said to be married, though no one had ever seen her husband—avoided me. She was always holding a book and isolating herself in its pages to avoid talking to her colleagues. Without planning it, we used to meet up in the teachers' lounge every Wednesday before noon. Just the two of us. We'd correct homework or prepare lessons. Pretty and silent. Throughout that free hour I felt the glow of her presence. I daydreamed about riding off in a four-by-four to a remote Amazonian forest accompanied by a captivating companion who held a Ph.D. in Hegelian philosophy, and equipped with the latest Japanese camera. When I invited her to the café, she gave an obscure smile and said, "Maybe later. Someday."

I ate, drank, read, and slept. Events unfolded but remained completely unaware. I'd become, in the words of the poet, "Neither like the sun nor like the moon." Depression revisited me, following years of absence amidst the tumultuous wars of that period. Even when nearby explosions went off, I ceased to ask who launched them. I withdrew completely. I had no appetite, and I came down with a light and persistent vertigo. I started walking all alone, wandering through the streets. I'd go down Independence Boulevard, then proceed up Three Moons Street before making a turn onto General Giraud Street. I didn't stop to sit in a café; I didn't stop at all, for I was not alone on this journey of mine. I found myself leading a procession that included figures like Prince Myshkin, Nicolai Stavroguine, Smerdyakov, and others afflicted with epilepsy or deadly tuberculosis. They shared a relentless passion for gambling, risking all their money, winning, and never stopping until they had lost it all. Some harbored a constant desire for self-destruction. These were individuals whom people claimed had a primal psychological craving for suffering, and they refused to relent until they teetered on the brink of death. On other days the procession would swell, and those run-down Slavic souls would be joined by a group of people from my hometown, which we left and never returned to—my relatives who had some relation through their father or their mother to the Sabbagh family. The math teacher who decided one day to smash all the mirrors in his house as though he were smashing his own image inside them. The beautiful woman in her forties who sometimes bathed in the cistern that was used to irrigate the orchards and would let down her long black hair and walk naked under the light of the moon. She'd call out to the men, and they would flee from her in fear.

The young man, who spent his days conversing with the deceased among the tombstones, addressing them by name and humorously recalling their past errors. And the twins from the summer village also filed into the ranks, and my martyred friend from the Arab Trotskyists Organization walked with us, too—he and all the members of that international cell. My mother tagged along as well, at the end of the procession. Characters from divergent times whose voices I could almost hear converged upon me, whispered in my ears. I'd pick up my pace, steal a swift glance over my shoulder, and start panting and sweating, my heart racing faster and faster, until I reached my house.

Until I reached my mother, who, shortly after her initial venture into the streets, confronted her fears once again. This time she journeyed far away. We found her clothes strewn all over the bed, as if she'd had trouble finding what she wanted to wear before disappearing. We sat speechless for an entire hour. Then my father left the house without telling me where he was going. I think he felt guilty. He came back early in the evening hoping to find that she had returned. The phone rang. It was my father's friend, the civil registrar, informing us in an erratic tone that my mother had made her way to them—he had no idea how—and she was going to spend the night. He advised my father to come get her in the morning. He said only that she was not okay.

A taxi had taken her to the town of our birth. She'd headed directly to her family's abandoned house in the old neighborhood. After her parents died and her sister ran away, the house had transformed into a skeleton of stone bricks. Thorns and weeds had grown inside the concrete and turned into a breeding ground for stray cats. She stood inside what was left of the room she had shared with her sister and began singing the childhood songs she had learned at the nuns' school, her voice ringing out loudly, songs that talk about the king's horse and the blond curls of the little girl waiting beneath the willow tree near the stream. Passersby heard her voice. They gathered at the front door of the house, and she continued singing. They recognized her and sought out the civil registrar, her husband's closest friend.

We arrived the next day. My father was confused, not knowing how to explain his wife's behavior to his friends. We brought her back home. I sat next to her in the back seat of the car and hugged her close to me the whole ride. She was sobbing quietly and whispering to me about the transience of the past. People go and houses fall to ruin. Emotions die, and fragrances die. She asked me how to bring them back. Why couldn't she go back to the years of mutual love with my father, to school, to the bosom of her parents and childhood when she had no concern about death, when she didn't know death existed? My quiet, well-behaved mother, satisfied with her lot, now seemed like a different woman I'd never met who was screaming to me for help. I couldn't bear her weakness. I tried to quiet her. Her words were rapping on the door to my heart.

After she settled down and my father and I started planning out how we would watch over her in shifts, I began exploring the surrounding neighborhoods looking for a coffee shop to frequent. I found it in a small semi-enclosed square. The following day I purchased an expensive notebook and a fountain pen, hoping that the quality of the paper and ink might imbue my words with greater meaning. I took a seat at a table that offered a view of the busy street teeming with cars. The first day I drank espresso and smoked cigarettes. It was an inaugural session in a spot with a view of the façade of a modern building and an adjacent kiosk selling newspapers and lottery tickets. I didn't write a single word. It sufficed merely to affirm my determination to begin writing, even though the exact form of the work remained unclear to me. I had the feeling that I was brimming with things I could say, and all I had to do was find the right wording for them. Then, one day, without prior planning, and without any noteworthy event prompting it, the words surged forth with such intensity that I found myself struggling to organize them, akin to water suddenly gushing from a dry spring in the middle of May when the rocky aquifer that feeds it unexpectedly erupts. Ten days to produce two pages.

The day following my burst of inspiration, I dried up. Just as I was beginning to enjoy a brief respite from the ruckus of my friendly ghosts, my maternal aunt came back—she who had eloped with a married man and disappeared without a trace. She had no one else to turn to but us.

She returned from Yamoussoukro by plane to Cyprus and from there to Lebanon by ferry, a trip during which she experienced torment with her son, especially at sea between Larnaca and Jounieh. My father didn't know who she was when she came through the door. She'd cut her hair short and dyed it two bright colors and was wearing a flower print dress. She'd done everything to make herself look young. Even her accent had changed during her years away, and her Arabic wasn't very clear. An adolescent came in with her, who was black. Characteristically African, with tightly curled hair and full lips. He didn't leave his mother's side, as though he were in enemy territory. He kept quiet, but if he answered a question posed to him by one of the grownups, he answered in French. I had come home from the Good Shepherd and found my aunt's luggage stacked up at the entrance to the apartment and my mother showering her sister with kisses while remaining a bit reserved towards the boy. Him she did not embrace and spoke to him from a distance. We gathered around my aunt to hear her story. She spoke right in front of her son, which was surprising to me. She shared the story of her encounter with her husband in that town that slept at sunset due to safety concerns. She described him as a charming man she had difficulty resisting, being a young girl who'd never been kissed by a boy in her life. His married life was filled with never-ending arguments and unbearable screaming, so he proposed running away with my aunt. He declared that whether she joined him or not, he was going. He scraped some money together and she sold her gold bracelets and necklace. They flew to Togo, and from there to Ghana, then Abidjan before settling down in the middle of Ivory Coast in Yamoussoukro. She was crazy in love with him while working by his side in the world of commerce. They lived through the tribal revolutions and the diamond wars and eventually they were blessed with a son.

I interrupted her to ask if they had gotten married. She recounted for us how a Catholic priest performed their wedding ceremony without asking them anything about their past.

Back then, when she got pregnant, the Yamoussoukro hospital had just received an ultrasound machine. The test showed that she was carrying a boy. Her husband was over-joyed. The baby in the womb kicked a lot, so he would press his ear against her belly to listen to the baby's movements. He kept watch over my aunt through the night, went with her to the hospital the day she gave birth, and when they brought the boy to her in the hospital room, her husband was shocked when he saws he was black. Skin color does not show up on an ultrasound. He almost fainted but steadied himself, then flew into a fit of rage, screaming and cursing in the hospital corridor, directly confronting the doctor and accusing him of swapping his son. The doctor walked him to the nursery where they place the newborn babies and said, "Look, there is not a single white baby among them."

The man didn't go back to his wife's room, or back to the house. That very night, his overwhelming anger struck him down with a fatal heart attack. My aunt faced hard-ships, and eventually she decided to leave Ivory Coast after enduring three robberies and growing concerned about her son's safety. Gradually, she sold everything and came back.

I raised the question once more of whether this boy was my aunt's son. His mother chuckled and gave him a hug. She told us everything while the question lingered in our minds: Where did this little black boy come from? My aunt provided no clue or hint to us. She spoke about him as her legitimate child. The befuddlement came from my parents as they observed the child and compared him to my aunt's hair and appearance.

The next day I took the boy into town. With him in tow, my appearance became even more mysterious. We sat at the café like two old friends. I ordered him a bowl of ice cream, raspberry flavored, while the customers and passersby stared at us—me and my cane and my cousin—with looks of astonishment.

The house became crowded with all of us. My parents and I, even when my paternal aunt was still alive, were silent types; that was just how God made us. I could no longer bear my parents' failing. Their childishness was clearly exposed in front of me, and I'd come to feel I was more grown up than them. And so, I turned a new page and left.

CHAPTER ON WOMEN

I CHECKED INTO Beryt Sur Mer—the ten-room hotel
I chanced upon while flipping through the tourist guide
to the capital city's attractions. Its façade was sky blue, its
windows white, and its proprietor's eyes green, inherited
from her Circassian mother. She'd renovated the building
with her husband. It had been built during the French
mandate, and for years, ever since the "official" end of the
war, it attracted small business owners who were misled
by the name and ended up complaining about the slow
service. Foreign journalists swarmed in whenever there
were kidnappings or assassinations that brought the war's
violence back into broad daylight. In their articles they
raved about the local arak and the tabbouleh and the *Sheikh
al-Mahshi*—eggplant casserole. The husband-and-wife
team also drew in tourists who'd read testimonials about
Beirut's indescribable magic. I brought two suitcases of
clothes, two canes, a selection of books I hadn't read yet,
my periods of melancholy, and the painting of Antar Bin
Shaddad, who glared at me, criticizing me for constantly

carting him away. I settled into a spacious corner room with two windows that overlooked Armenia Street and ate up half my monthly teacher's salary in rent, even after the generous discount I got for being a permanent guest. Breakfast could be taken in a little courtyard, but the guests fled back inside, away from all the mosquitoes that flew around the place year-round no matter the season.

I took up sitting in the lobby during my free time away from schoolwork. I kept my back to the wall and my writing journal in front of me, even though I'd stopped opening it, striving to uncover every little detail of the place: by eavesdropping on the man sitting alone at the bar who kept snapping his fingers and ordering successive drinks of vodka with pomegranate juice; by reading the names of old songs recorded on the defunct jukebox in the corner; by observing the owner of the hotel, who crossed the lobby carrying carpentry tools to fix the doors and the sinks, paint the walls, and sketch birds of strange colors and bouquets of flowers on them while his wife sat flaunting her beauty to the guests.

Sometimes I'd go check on my mother. She hardly talked anymore, and her eyes wandered. If asked a question, she'd answer with a belabored smile and say she was perfectly fine, but she wouldn't talk at all if unprompted. My aunt sat across from her, silently wondering what had come over her sister. I'd ask my mother again about my father, and she'd say she had no idea. He no longer came home for lunch. He had a lot of work. She didn't say it with the same sarcasm as before. She'd lost the energy to complain.

I'd take my cousin to the nearby café for ice cream, surrounded by prying eyes. I was trying to make it up to him for the bullying he received at school where they called him names, as he told me, and made jungle animal sounds at him. In class, he sat all alone at a desk meant for two students. They backed away from him, held their noses and said he smelled. He came home crying every day. I headed to the school under the pretense of having an appointment with the principal, strode past the gatekeeper and snuck into his classroom. I forcefully flung the door open, making the teacher quiver in fear. The boy came running to me. I yelled at the students in a menacing and stern tone, telling them to quit harassing him, and I threatened them that if he came home crying again, I would punish the guilty party—because I knew everything and the names of all the culprits, so they had better watch out, and I left. He got a break from them, for a little while. Back at home they told me that two young men had come by asking for me while I was out. They'd left a phone number for me to call them back.

I discovered amid my preoccupation with the guests in the lobby how the faces of the lodgers changed. There was the guy with the long hair and open sandals who appeared with his bag slung over his shoulder. He spent the night hopping through the bars, stumbled back to the hotel inebriated, and disappeared the next day headed for Damascus. Two young European women came along, blonde and blue-eyed. The hotel owner gave me a dubious look hinting they were lovers. They checked into a room together for the weekend, had their breakfast there, and only came out for lunch. There was a fat guy with an Egyptian accent who laughed boisterously at his own jokes as he commented on current events and conversed with the television. His stay didn't last very long. I'd go back to my white sheet of paper, make an attempt at writing, erase it, rip it up, and then I noticed there was one guest who never left. A man in his seventies who'd get up in the morning, shower, shave, and spend a long time standing in front of his closet before choosing the clothes that best suited his mood, though the vast majority were white or various shades thereof. Anyone who saw him tie a napkin around his neck while taking his first sip of red wine and nodding his head in delight while savoring chocolate knew that over the course of his long life, he had sampled numerous kinds of pleasures. A burly young man used to come to visit him. He liked to show off his muscles and tattoos. Many days passed when the seventy-year-old never left the hotel. Early in the week, we would find ourselves the only remaining lodgers, and so we became friends. He had owned a gold and jewelry shop in the old downtown area of the capital, which was reduced to ashes in a single night during the civil war, and had managed to salvage some of his business. He told me all about his experience. "Every time we witnessed a bit of prosperity, someone would come along to take a share of it and tear down what we'd built."

I decided not to embark on a discussion with him in which I didn't know who "we" were and who "they" were. Then he whispered to me that the hotel proprietress was shooting occasional glances towards me. He said she was an easy catch, and she was definitely concealing some problem or other.

"I wouldn't advise you to prolong the matter with her. With an unhappily married woman, as soon as she gets used to you, she'll start moaning and complaining. Her secret love affair will remind her of everything she missed out on in her youth. She'll become a burden for you that you won't know how to unload."

And that's exactly what happened. The hotel house-keeper didn't come in to work one day, so the owner came knocking at my door volunteering to change the sheets herself. She encouraged me to stay in the room since it wouldn't take long. She started making dance moves, bending over the bed to yank the big white sheet into the air and then gather it up by the corners with skill, changing the pillowcases, wiggling her butt and talking, asking me why I had a cane at such a young age. A refreshing breeze blew in through the open window overlooking the noisy street. She knelt on top of the bed to tuck in the corners and removed her shoes. The sound of them dropping to the floor was a signal to me, so I approached to help her from the other side. We couldn't help touching, but neither of us tried to move away. On the contrary, we clutched each other even more, and then I made a move. I kissed her neck deeply, and she moaned in delight loudly enough to be heard at the sidewalk cafés outside. We dropped onto the bed for an entire hour, after which she changed the linens again and waited for the redness to fade from her cheeks and neck and arms before rushing down to her desk in the lobby. It was obvious from her expertise and preparations that that wasn't her first time.

I have no idea how my friend the hotel resident knew about our little tryst. The next afternoon he interrupted my losing battle with writing, ordered me a glass of wine, and immediately started accusing me of having nothing wrong with my leg. He'd been observing me closely and could tell I had no need for the cane. I liked his perceptiveness, so

I told him my story. He told me that the most pleasant encounters happened in hotels. He added that he could read faces and recited a line of poetry.

> I recognize lovers by their glances, and I see those satisfied femme fatales within them with their charms and wiles.

He'd experienced women. He'd become good at befriending them and knew their weaknesses and desires, with the exception of his much younger wife, who insisted on a divorce after catching him cheating on her and after getting sick and tired of washing and ironing his white clothes. Truly, all of his clothes were white—his shirts, his pants, his socks—so they got dirty quickly, plus he wouldn't wear anything two days in a row. They'd pile up and fill his wife with loathing at the sight of them. He had a theory about that: "If you want to find the secret behind marital infidelity, search in gold and jewelry. There were nine women for every man who came in to see us at the jewelry shop."

He'd ended up alone. His son went off to work for a company in New York City and never called. He owned a comfortable house, but he refused to live there all alone and miserable, relying on hired help to feed him, so years ago he decided to move into the hotel. He enjoyed the vagabond life there. He wouldn't be leaving behind any inheritance— not property or money. When he eventually lost his ability to take care of himself, he would put an end to his life. He was preparing the best possible scenario for that inevitable day. I think one reason he liked me was because I didn't try to make him change his mind about that plan of his.

He warned me about my relationship with the proprietress and said that her husband often made rounds through the rooms and might catch us and discover our little game. The husband was an upright and just man, and because he was upright and just, his anger might be formidable. And he was always carrying sharp metal tools in his hands. My friend thought the husband was neglecting his wife in bed, most likely due to some impotence on his end or because she was the type who couldn't be satisfied.

"He might take out his frustration over being impotent on you and on her. Within the human psyche is a myriad of complexes. As my mother used to say, 'It's safer to dwell in the heart of a lion than in the heart of a man.'"

I never feared any potential threat to myself. From my early days in adolescence, amidst the turmoil of my town, where danger whispered to me in secret and I responded, I have consistently gravitated toward danger instead of fleeing from it. Later on, I thought about my old comrades, so I called them at the number they'd left for me. A voice on the other end of the phone asked me tersely if I was still honoring the pledge of revolution with my comrades. I heard myself answering yes without thinking. He conveyed to me that I should expect to receive some encoded messages at the hotel where I was staying and hung up without saying goodbye. Actually, I had distanced myself from the ideas of Leon Trotsky in favor of reembracing the sufferings of Goethe, but I didn't want to lose my friendship with the comrades, so I waited for their message. A few days later the hotel owner yelled to me with a tone that was both mocking and admonishing, "A love letter for the man with the refined taste."

The comment about refined taste comment was directed at the girl who'd dropped by the hotel to deliver the letter and whose beauty had drawn the proprietress's attention. The proprietress read the letter and assumed that the mail carrier had written it. In an effort to protect their clandestine activity—whose covertness no one gave a damn about as long as there were weapons in everyone's hands, and firing them hardly required an excuse while the militias controlled the neighborhoods and the crossings—the comrades came to the agreement that the genuine messages were meant to be composed initially and subsequently wrapped within another message, bearing a similar but misleading meaning, to deceive the reader. In this message, it was a declaration of longing and infatuation, signed with a woman's name and written in a school-composition style and overflowing with phony emotions.

I pored over the letter with a glass of vodka with lemon, deciphering the encoded message. The last letter of the first word followed by the second-to-last letter of the second word, etc. Tactics the propagandists of the permanent international revolution liked to utilize during the tyrannical rule of the czars. After a bit of strain, I extracted from the love letter the following message: "At any cost and without delay, remove the one who tops the list of the rich who was commissioned to rebuild the capital city. He is going to push the country into a revenue-generating economy, crush the poor, and stick us with barbarous globalism."

I had seen that wealthy businessman on television many times. He'd seemed to me like a nice and generous man. I coaxed my co-lodger at the hotel over to talk about him, and we agreed that unlike the majority of influential people, he seemed trustworthy. My buddy told me stories about him in his youth and how he was a self-made man, how he visited his elderly mother once a week in the village that she never left, kissed her hand, and did charitable deeds in her name. But people don't like the rich, especially the ones who flaunt their wealth all over the place.

I received the second letter, handed to me by the hotel owner, with even more contempt this time. In it they asked me to follow the man's news in the media, track his movements, write them down. I wasn't sure what to do. I sat to write a reply that took me hours to word correctly, superficially expressing rejection for the purported romance. I declined and said that I was involved with a woman with green eyes, luscious lips, and a curvaceous body, whom I'd never be unfaithful to and wouldn't trade for anyone. With that, I satisfied the owner's ego because she would undoubtedly read that surface message. On the other hand, I was extending a revolutionary salute to my comrades via the disguised text of the letter and was telling them that I was busy with other matters and was too far away from the specified target.

Then I lost my line of communication with the cell. My letter ended up staying with the owner of the hotel because the girl didn't come by to pick it up and no one deciphered its code. The smile returned to the owner's face, and she said she was going to keep the letter as a beautiful souvenir from me and would never give it away. Two days later, while I was in the reception area busily grading semester exams from school, a video clip appeared on the lobby television that aired on mute throughout the day, showing a young man dressed in a new suit and necktie. He stood just like the Serbian Gavrilo Princip when he assassinated Archduke Franz Ferdinand and set off the Great War, as was said. The young man on TV pulled out his revolver and emptied its bullets into the front door window on the driver's side of the car where he assumed the businessman was seated. Then he raised his hands in the air in surrender and remained in that posture until a couple of officers from the Internal Security motorcycle unit arrived to arrest him. The business tycoon wasn't hit because he had been riding in the car at the end of the convoy, and people also said he was driving. I felt bad about the failure that dogged the Arab Trotskyists and their schemes, and I also felt relieved that the man came out of it unscathed, and then, to my delight, the philosophy teacher finally came out of her silent bubble.

Luring her in was easy. I asked her opinion on marriage and out came her secret. She looked all around and said that she couldn't tell me much about that because she wasn't married and lived with her mother and her books, too. She wore a ring on her finger and spread the word that she was married to keep men away from her. Nonetheless, she still kept up her beautiful appearance. She powdered her cheeks to brighten up the paleness of her face, which was reminiscent of the women of Delacroix.

The women that I associated with took me far away from myself, to the mythology that dwelled inside me, whereas my mother dragged me back to where I started: to the morning humidity from the river that spilled into the houses and caused achy joints; to the math teacher who walked on tiptoes; and to the father of my childhood friend wiping his sweat on a hot summer evening and arguing with his wife about lineage, my lineage. She fought off her destiny as best she could with what means she had available—a kind of madness that would draw blood from herself but not harm others.

I saved the philosophy teacher for later. I postponed my entrance into her world until I could take care of my other concerns—going to see my mother, sitting beside her, breathing in the smell of her, and trying to pull her up out of that deep plummet she'd taken into herself. My funny stories didn't make her laugh no matter how hard I tried. She was somewhere else, hiding from the present. She looked straight ahead without seeing her sister imposing her ways on the house, decorating the walls with African dolls, and didn't hear her chiding her son in French. My aunt offered to pay a share of the rent, but my father refused. She relieved my mother from cooking. She made spicy dishes from Ivory Coast that had strange names. She tried to root herself in our house since she could never step foot in our hometown again. Over there she would be easy prey for their malice. She would be blamed for her husband's death, and they would mock her for the little boy clinging to her. They'd consider him a punishment to her for "snatching" a man away from his wife and his daughter. She took on all the domestic responsibilities while my mom just took care of the lilies on the porch and her yellow roses. And every now and then she would write—in the blank pages of the Bible or in the margins. I don't know what prompted me to flip through her Bible when I found it there on the couch. I had wanted to reread Christ's Sermon on the Mount and pore over sayings whose meanings remained foggy to me, such as "Blessed are the poor in spirit, for theirs is the kingdom of heaven; Blessed are the meek, for they shall inherit the earth."

I found that my mother had written, in a slow, crooked hand, a supplication to the Virgin Mary asking her to cast upon me her blue cloak and protect me from the fates. And in the margin beside the chapter about the resurrection of Lazarus, she had written in fine, microscopic script:

> *My father was afraid of death and feared that there was no God. The day he died he asked me while he lay there in bed with labored breaths what I believed. I panicked and became tongue-tied. Then he said, "Let's believe he's there waiting for us," and closed his eyes for all eternity.*

As was his habit, my own father was spending a lot of time away from the house. I wasn't sure if he'd gotten caught up in another affair. I passed by his work and saw him there all dressed up, his shiny hair well-combed, whispering in the ear of a young woman who let out a boisterous laugh, so I hurried back home to the hotel—only to find two security officers in military uniform waiting for me. They swiftly took me in to the police station to give my testimony. When I got there, I found most of the members of the cell there too. We greeted each other warmly with kisses. One of the men at the station had some unexpected criticism for us.

"You're a bunch of cowards. You can't be counted on for anything. For this big operation you sent out a guy who can't shoot."

I realized at that point that the war hadn't ended. It had merely changed form. We didn't deny knowing the gunman. I mentioned to the investigator that the gunman was a stubborn man who never strayed from his principles. But we had been unanimous in stating we had taken no part in the assassination attempt. And from the moment he was arrested, the suspect told the interrogators repeatedly that he had planned and acted alone. They had found our names in his phone contacts. They accused us of being associated with an armed gang and detained us together in the police station jail. We chanted,

"Build your castles on the farmlands
From our toil and the work of our hands
Let your dogs loose in the streets
And lock your cell doors on us"

We reminisced and shared our news before they let us go due to the difficulty of feeding us and finding beds for all of us in the small jail, and also because they couldn't pin any nefarious acts on us, so they let us out on bond. Our pictures appeared on the inside pages of the newspapers the next day, with us standing huddled in a circle, me in the center leaning on my cane. We looked like a basketball team. We got off easy because the target had enemies in high government positions. We played the game of chicken with them to see who would hold out the longest, and I heard whispers that an intelligence agency had managed to turn one of the head officers of the cell and ordered him to carry out that ill-fated assassination attempt. Two lawyers volunteered to represent us pro bono, and they succeeded in halting the investigation. Our pact was dissolved, and only two or three of us were left to drag along the revolutionary name.

My colleagues at school found out about what happened and began whispering about me. They looked me up and down as if rediscovering my appearance. The philosophy teacher wanted to know if I'd read *Das Kapital* and if I was a believer in the dialectic of history. The news reached the hotel, too. The hotel owner wanted to win me back. She cornered me and we hurried to my room, but after a little while her husband bellowed from the hallway, calling her name. I stopped but she persisted, as if his presence right outside the door excited her. She whispered in my ear that he'd leave in a few minutes and that he believed whatever she told him. She concluded with a strong declaration, firmly stating, "Anyhow, he doesn't have control over me."

I told my hotel lodger friend what happened, which convinced him once and for all that the man was impotent. He said that the rumors about me had probably turned her on. That's how women were. As for at my folks' house, there was no trace of newspapers and no following of news reports over there. I discovered that my mother's condition was worsening. She'd get dressed and go sit in the parlor from morning to night, eating very little despite repeated attempts to persuade her to eat. I decided to take her to a doctor. He examined her privately for nearly an hour, and when she came out, he called me over and said he was going to prescribe some medication for her to give her a little boost because she was suffering from deep nostalgic depression. He also recommended trying to provide some recreation for her. I passed along the doctor's orders to my aunt, and she mentioned having a homemade potion she had learned from the people in Africa. I emphasized not to leave my mother alone and gave her my phone number at the hotel. Later, we came to realize that my mother was feigning taking the medication and secretly stashing it in her bedroom closet.

During that time, the young German journalist from *Frankfurter Zeitung* passed through town like a meteor. By chance, the service staff put her in the room next to mine, but before she could settle in, the hotel owner moved her to another floor, claiming that the room had already been booked. She exerted a lot of effort to keep us apart, but we had already spoken to each other before she'd arrived. That evening, we were excited to pick up our conversation. We savored German literature together under the gaze of the disgruntled proprietress. My way of winning women's hearts was tried and true. I lamented that life was a deceptive illusion, where I bore the weight of my dreams, and that my letdowns followed me no matter where I ventured or made a home. She was blonde and broad-shouldered, with a camera that never left her side. I toured with her through the gloom and the sewers in the alleys of Sabra and Shatila refugee camps. We noted the pictures of hundreds of victims pasted on the dirty walls while a crowd of children followed us, having been intrigued by the presence of a blonde woman in that place. From there, we made our way to the new city center, surrounded by grand luxury buildings, with the blue sea, and the vibrant lilac trees. She was always hunting for contradictions. A displaced old man in front of a Christian Dior shop or a building carrying scars of the war and the passage of time right beside a new bank with its shiny glass storefront. On the way back to the hotel, we talked about Beirut and the phoenix, about Lebanon and the myth of Sisyphus and other simple metaphors. She went up to her room and I slipped in after her. In bed we touched each other to the rhythm of the "Drummer Boy Story," and we exchanged kisses to the whispers of German poetry. She would erupt in fits of wild laughter exclaiming, "I must be dreaming," and then rub her eyes to wake herself up. She involved me in her exploration of the capital. She brought me back to the city center to take pictures of me standing there, looking into the distance, leaning against the Martyrs' statue. It had been restored and placed back in the exact spot the fighters had removed it from. She told me before she left that she would write an article with the title, "Me and Heinrich Heine and the Handsome Teacher in Bed in Beirut." The managing editor of the newspaper would love it. She sent a clipping from the German paper to Beryt Sur Mer after I'd left the hotel. I imagine the owner found someone to translate it for her, which would have heightened her disappointment and reinforced her belief in the wickedness of men. She'd set sex aside and turn to her husband as a secure friend who could shield her from the treachery of those wanderers passing through an inn that claimed to overlook the sea but overlooked nothing but a street clamoring with car mechanic shops and cheap cafés.

While I was engaged in all of this, a persistent feeling nagged at me—the sense that I was neglecting the writing that I'd left home for, which held the promise of a cohesive world where I held the reins, away from life's bitterness and all its inequalities. But it seemed there were others waiting for me, especially women, ready to feed greedily on my life, planting their seeds in it and distributing the harvest among themselves. I could only manage to add a few pages to the diary I'd started in the café about the progression of the days and the colors of the seasons, feelings I'd gathered about a character—a young man overwhelmed by the withering of the violet tree or the looks of early heartbreak in the eyes of a young girl. Filled with worry, he observes from his window as children play with a boomerang, tossing it into the air, waiting for it to return to them. He dreams of ridding himself of his books because he wants to combat life naked, without help, eye-to-eye. A compilation of fragile details that might tell more about me than the deeds of the revolutionary cell or my successive adventures during the season of women who pounced on me, one after the other, at Beryt Sur Mei. Winning women over was easy for me in that transit hotel, where they were far away from their familiar defenses, where I seemed to blend in seamlessly with the environment. Sometimes I simplified the enigmas of the East for them in their native language. In my turn, I took them as a mantle to drape over myself, prolonging my distraction from the black hole in my life. A tall Swedish woman who was studying the Arabic language in books but wanted to hear it from the mouths of its native speakers... she came to Beirut and stood there bewildered before the hieroglyphics of the "language of the letter *Ḍād.*" She approached the painting of Antar in my room, ran her fingers over the letters of the lines from the *Mu'allaqa* and said there was no doubt the Muslims were right when they said that God revealed the Quran in Arabic. A French woman of Moroccan origin who'd been born in a Paris suburb... I would translate the words from Umm Kulthum songs for her while we lay naked under the covers, making her feel she'd returned to roots of hers, even if she didn't know what those roots were. A Turkish archeologist who was taking part in the excavation of Roman ruins in Beirut … We settled for intimate meetings in the reception hall. She didn't drink alcohol, didn't invite me to her room. I suspect she was keeping pottery pieces from her digs that she planned to secretly take back with her to Istanbul.

My short-lived relationships, in which my role was more like that of an adulterer, led the hotel owner to abandon any hope of weaving a romantic tale with me. I don't know what illusion she was chasing by clinging so tightly to me, or what kind of future she as a married woman was painting for this dalliance with a much younger man. She no longer paid me any attention and openly engaged in hushed conversations with her husband, who appeared to notice my presence, even though I avoided making eye contact with him to avoid drawing his attention. A few days later, my buddy, the hotel resident, came to me in his white clothes and a red tie. We went for a walk outside, and he shared that the hotel owner's husband wanted me to know I wasn't welcome at the hotel anymore. He didn't want his home or his hotel to be destroyed.

"His wife told him that you were hitting on her. She's jealous and wants to punish you for all those affairs of yours right and left."

Just like that, the "Beryt Sur Mer dish" got burned. Its milk turned sour. I couldn't imagine any other cosmopolitan hotel that might take me in at the time, which coincided with my mother's new complaints of head pain that regular sedatives couldn't alleviate. I told my buddy to ask the hotel owner to give me a week to figure something out.

THE TEMPORARY ASSYRIAN

THINGS MOVED QUICKLY. The philosophy teacher and I at Good Shepherd High School had been passing through an air gap and just needed a helping hand to pull us up. I left the Armenia Street hotel upon my co-lodger friend's insistence and went back to live with my parents. I spent time with my mom, encouraged her to talk, but she didn't say much. She was wilting, dying in our arms, and we didn't know how to hold onto her. We'd go see the doctor and he wouldn't find anything concerning healthwise in the various lab tests he ordered. She, on the other hand, was keenly aware of her condition and knew exactly what was in store. She gave my aunt instructions:

"When I go, look after my husband and my son."

When my aunt, trying to lighten the mood, asked her where she wanted to go, a wry smile appeared on my mother's face.

The idea of marriage was not on either of our minds when we went out together, my school colleague and I, walking along the streets and maintaining our ongoing conversation. We were two abstract thinkers. We carried on a discussion around the literary knowledge that I relied on for monitoring the manifestations of the world and its secrets, and philosophy—the crown of the sciences, as she called it. I never asked about her family or where she was born. I preferred her to be of unknown origins, to have come from nowhere, and she in turn showed little interest in the story of my life before we crossed paths. We wandered inside a bubble of ideas as though we'd just emerged from the womb of books. She didn't like cafés. She couldn't stand the idleness of the men who sat with their fat bellies protruding in front of them. So we would walk, and before we parted ways we would promise to pick it up the next day, the never-ending discussion we'd randomly started, dredging up ideas from everywhere. Truly, we were engaged in a spectacular cultural competition in which we lobbed the names of experts and titles of books, not to mention quotes that we cited from memory in support of our ideas. We compensated in words for our bodily distance. No kisses, no holding hands, no caresses. I took pains to hold back and keep some space between us. I even apologized if we ever brushed against each other unintentionally, which would bring out a smile on her face that said she understood my game. I promised myself that our story would be unique, that we would be spared the dullness of repetition. We persevered through nearly two months of gearing up. Conversations and short outings. We put off the celebration of our bodies and reveled in the pouring out of our ideas until I made the stupidest mistake of my life.

We were walking down Sursock Street, past a palace from the Ottoman period hidden behind the Japanese cherry trees, when I paused and addressed her in a formal manner with an exaggerated tone.

"Would you accept, dear lady, to take up residence with me?"

Her answer was quick and in the same tone:

"You must know, if the matter is of concern to you, that I do not consider marriage to be a sacred bond."

I chuckled in turn and said in all honesty that I agreed with her on that opinion.

She told her mother that I was an only child, handsome and cultured. I don't know which of those descriptors was most convincing, but her mother agreed on the condition that we get married "legally in the eyes of God." A few days later she asked me, "Where would you like us to live?"

Her question brought us down to earth, to the ground that we had been hovering over. After all her fervor for Hegelian idealism and my unique blend of dialectic Marxism and abstract poetic creativity, we switched gears and delved into comparing the expenses of renting a house within and outside the city limits. We vied with each other over our choices for the brand of washing machine, too, or the stove. We'd agree and then disagree. Mostly we disagreed. About there being two separate bedrooms—one for each of us, while we discussed what her mother's fate would be without her. The trivialities multiplied, as did the petty clashes. I don't know which moment, which little detail caused the poison of discord to come between us. That black cloud came back to hover over my head. When the world offered me joy, I turned obstinate, a stubborn mule refusing to budge, so the days had to drag me along by force.

121

It came time to make wedding arrangements. We agreed, like two balanced, intelligent people who didn't like showing off and didn't want to go overboard with a big celebration, to limit it to family and close friends. The only things she was adamant about were the white wedding dress and having two children to walk behind her, holding her train. She proposed that, from my side of the family, we should involve my little African cousin, before pulling a new rabbit out of her hat.

"I'm Muslim," she said.

There was nothing in her first name or her family name that gave any indication of her religion. Both of her names were good for any denomination in these lands of the Holy Books. It was in contrast to me, who'd been dragging along the name of my father's father since birth—that of the most renowned of Jesus's disciples, the one who was crucified upside down because he considered himself unworthy of being put to death in the same manner as his master. She agreed to get married in church, but she refused to change her religion. She put up hurdles and I jumped over them. I told her that I didn't care if she wasn't a virgin and didn't care if she wasn't Christian. If she wanted, I was ready to walk over to the Ja'fari Court with her to draw up the marriage contract there.

When we approached the Maronite priest, he expressed regret that according to the latest Patriarchal recommendations he was not allowed to officiate the marriage ceremony between a Christian groom and a Muslim bride. The Shiite cleric did the same, so we resorted to seeking the services of the Assyrian sect, whose clergy accepted mixed marriage. I could adopt the Assyrian faith by merely answering yes to one question the bishop of Mount Lebanon would ask me, and after the wedding I could go back to what I was before, and she could stay as she was—a Twelver Shiite woman from the Baydoun neighborhood and resident of the capital Beirut.

My folks arrived at the church, a total of four individuals after the reinforcements coming from Ivory Coast, in a red taxi. My aunt had tied a big bunch of colorful balloons to the antenna. My father, true to character, appeared pleased with the bride's beauty. He gazed at her and then turned to me, nodding his head in approval of my excellent selection. My mother wore her nice outfit. She was displeased that I was marrying, despite all her efforts to stop me. The bride's relatives came in three cars. They whispered bitterly among themselves as they got out of the cars, waving their arms and arguing about the marriage most likely. There were two women among them wearing head coverings. One of them entered the church while the other wouldn't step foot in it and waited outside. It wasn't until that day that I learned that the bride's father was deceased and had been a well-known calligrapher. She brought a souvenir of his to our house, a framed piece of art on which he had written in geometric lettering, "The full stalks of grain bow down modestly, and the empty ones hold their heads up high."

A number of our colleagues from the Good Shephard showed up uninvited. The married ones brought their wives. They'd gotten suits and ties for the occasion. Before the start of the rituals, three comrades from the old revolutionary cell showed up. I have no idea how they heard about it or how they found the church. They clasped their hands behind their backs and stood near the door throughout the service, beside the font of holy water, so it wouldn't be counted against them as having visited the church. After all, they were believers in history and the evolutionary process rather than in a creator god. I went over to talk to them, and they told me that they were just friends now and that most of the members of the revolutionary cell had come to believe that our country got the economy it deserved. Some of them had even entered the world of business.

And so there we were, the Muslims and the heretics—the bridal couple included—forming the vast majority of people on that day inside Saint George's Assyrian Church near the National Museum. My best man arrived late. I had chosen my friend from Beryt Sur Mer to stand as my witness. I also harbored doubts about his religious affiliation until he eventually disclosed to me that he was Protestant. That was because his Orthodox-born father had been educated under the Evangelicals and adopted their faith in order to ensure a free education for his children at the American University in Beirut. We were about to replace him with a volunteer—one of the schoolteachers—but he came in panting minutes before the start of the service and said that the taxi driver got mixed up and took him to the Chaldean church on the other side of town. With the exception of the priest and his assistant with the mellow voice who haggled with me over the required payment, insisting that they had fixed prices for baptisms, funerals, and weddings, I was the only Assyrian—and a temporary one at that—among them. I put off returning to my original religion afterwards once I was told that it required complicated procedures that took years to complete, so I also became the only Assyrian in my town. "When the topic of obtaining a new Civil Registry Extract with my wife's name came up, the registrar, who was rumored to have delayed retirement by altering his date of birth and advancing it five years, recognized me and remarked, 'You're that communist. So, now you're an Assyrian? Please convey my regards to your father.'"

My cousin was the star of the wedding celebration. I imagined that his biological father might be a follower of animism and could have added even more variety to the multiple religions inside the little church at the wedding we had hoped would be intimate. The little girl the bride had picked to help carry the train of her wedding gown kept giving him fearful looks. She'd never been so close to a black person before that day. My mother remained seated throughout the ceremony, sighing in exhaustion. The bride asked the priest to read a passage from *The Prophet* by Kahlil Gibran that she had handwritten on a piece of paper. What the author, who himself had never married, said drew my attention.

But let there be spaces in your togetherness,
And let the winds of the heavens dance
between you.

The choice of that reading held a certain irony that only the coming days would reveal. Then the priest, perhaps because the bride and I came from two different sects, delivered a short sermon in which he spoke about the importance of living in harmony and embracing diversity as a fountain of cultural and social richness. Then, he touched upon the concept of Lebanon as "the Message" before we stepped outside, where a photographer moved around, organizing us into different arrangements." Afterwards we framed the picture and hung it in the kitchen of our new house next to my old picture of my paternal aunt and the dog and General De Gaulle. In the wedding picture was my maternal aunt in skimpy lightweight clothing suitable for the hot weather in Ivory Coast, and my friend from the hotel with his expensive cologne whispering in my ear, "If you'd asked me, I would not have advised marriage." He had fastened his bowtie and ensured that the handkerchief was visible by pulling it out from his jacket pocket. The philosophy teacher and I were in the middle of the group, smiling. The former revolutionary comrades who didn't care much for such occasions came wearing casual shirts and jeans. They stood before the camera lens, adhering to a tradition they typically held in low regard. Some of the bride's relatives had scowls on their faces. The women were in ample clothing and the men were in transition between the country and the city, most with moustaches and baggy sherwal pants or shirts without collars. A one-of-a-kind mix. That wedding day was the sole day of joy in that entire ordeal they call married life.

A life that began with the death of my mother. My father got up for work as usual. My cousin slung his backpack over his shoulder and headed out for the toils of school while his mother went off to do the shopping. My aunt would have regrets once again for leaving her sister alone, and I blamed myself because I knew my mother's death was imminent and didn't do everything in my power to save her. She went to her closet, took out the sedatives she had been hiding in there, and swallowed all of them. She put her feet up on the chair, propped her head with a pillow, threw a light blanket over herself, and went to sleep forever. She went to where she thought she would reunite with her innocence and with her parents.

My aunt came back from shopping, glimpsed my mother sitting in her usual place, and went directly to the kitchen with her grocery bags. She called to my mother from there, but my mother didn't answer. Recently, before that, that would happen all the time. She wouldn't answer even though she'd heard. So, my aunt busied herself making lunch. The silence in the living room was absolute. My aunt went in to check on my mother. She thought she was sleeping. She observed her face and its tense features. No doubt she had been in pain before surrendering her spirit. My aunt shook my mother's shoulders, and she toppled over. She wasn't breathing. My aunt let out a piercing scream that reverberated through every floor of the building before flinging open the door and dashing outside, hysterical. In her cry for help was a deep, African ululation. There was no way she would stay there by herself with her big sister slumped over motionless.

Similar to when we attended the wedding, a single car transported us to the town, but this time trailed by the funeral hearse. We performed the funeral prayers for her there in the presence of a crowd that had come to see us after our long absence. We buried her beside her father and mother, where she wished to be laid to rest. My wife was there, remaining silent the whole time. Her expression was stern both during the ride there and through the funeral. My aunt didn't dare accompany us. Her husband's family blamed her for his death. They incited the fury of his young daughter against my aunt and made threats to harm her.

The priest gave a eulogy in which he praised my mother's dedication to her family and her faithfulness, ignoring the circumstances of her death. We accompanied her to the cemetery against the custom of the townspeople, who only visited their dead once a year, at the start of November.

Upon our return to the capital, defeated, as the day drew to a close, I opened her New Testament and discovered that she had added something to the final page:

> *The sky is dark, and the devil reigns over the world. The rain will be confined as retribution to the sinners. The earthly paradise is childhood.*

For the second time in my adult life, I cried. I cried a lot. I waited for my wife to go off to school before I broke down in loud sobs. Bawling out loud like that, while walking from one end of the house that we finally chose as our residence to the other, gave me a great deal of relief. I think I was crying for my mother and also for myself. Even to this day, she lingers in my mind, with her forlorn gaze, as if she's silently pleading for help in a merciless sea, clutching onto some makeshift raft while the waves lap at her. I didn't take any of her effects except for the Bible and her hat with the black-and-yellow feather. When I read what she'd written, my anxiety turned into fear. Fear that the tendency towards ruin didn't come from what was happening to us in our daily lives, but from something we carry inside ourselves, without knowing when it will come to the surface and slip out of our control. And fear that my whole life up until that point had merely been an attempt to control that impending ruin. My mother and I had been bearing the burden together. Now that she was gone, I felt the weight of it tipping the scales to my side alone. I became fragile. My nerves would spill over at the smallest display of obstinance. I couldn't stand any deviousness at school. Adolescent pranks infuriated me. I'd shout in their faces so vehemently that the principal could hear me and would rush to mediate on my behalf. But one day, a student was imitating my accent while I was speaking as a genuine Frenchman, enunciating the 'r' like a 'gh' sound. It made his buddies laugh at me and initiated all sorts of clowning around. I waved my cane at him but stopped short of hitting him with it, satisfying myself with a hefty slap across his face that silenced the lecture hall. The principal called me in as a result, to give me a scolding. I resigned, in exchange for a generous severance package, leaving me with my writing aspirations and the interest from my paternal aunt's bank account, the principal of which I still hadn't touched.

The real estate agent took us into the distant outskirts. The rents in Beirut skyrocketed. The city kicked us all the way out to the edge of the eastern suburbs. The further away we went from the city center, the lower the rent. We ended up in a first-floor apartment with a pine tree out front whose trunk drooped in sorrow. It had managed to survive the building frenzy that crept its way up the hills surrounding the capital. I remembered what my walker friend had said about the eastern suburbs absorbing the newcomers to the city who came from the Christian countryside. Here we were making a liar out of him— taking off to the suburbs from the heart of the capital with our load of books and artwork in tow, a Shiite, and a Maronite-turned-Assyrian.

We opted for a renovated house with a modified floor design. Two bedrooms and a big space that, from the very first day, we disagreed on how to furnish. I can't explain how our shared living situation transformed into an epic of unending conflict. She disapproved of the painting of Antar and Abla, considering it naive, so I hung it on my bedroom wall. She also dismissed the notion of a pool table and two leather Chesterfield couches. Leather was too cold, and billiards didn't interest her in the least. She liked carpeting and heavy drapes and darkness while I preferred light and wide-open spaces. In the end, we agreed to let each one decorate their own bedroom however they liked and we decided to leave the big living room bare until we could come to a mutual agreement on how to furnish it. While waiting for that, if I happened to bring a chair into that room to sit on, I'd come back home later to find that she'd dragged it out to the balcony or the kitchen. We'd argue a little and then cool down. But after my mom died, we started arguing about everything. Every suggestion and every color choice. We'd dodge each other at school, and when it came time to go back to classes in the fall, she transferred to another school, and I quit teaching. She bought a car with her own savings without telling me. Our marriage had remained white for more than a month. I wasn't in a hurry. We had sex a few times, often following a heated argument. It would nearly come to blows and I wouldn't rest until I'd destroyed some precious object of hers. A crystal vase from her trousseau, or our wedding picture, which I shattered in one of those fits of anger and hurled off the balcony onto the main street, where the passing cars' tires erased any evidence of it. Despite all that, sometimes the situation ended up in her bedroom, devoid of passion, merely a fulfilment of our marital duties. Afterwards, I would spend the night alone in my bedroom, contented. We ate ready-made meals with no flavor and rarely met up at the kitchen table. Words between us seeped away. We got by on curt utterances about mundane practical matters. One day while I was standing at a street corner waiting for a taxi to the bookstore that I'd been frequenting, I saw her drive by. I think she saw me too, but she turned her face in the other direction. She wasn't alone. A man was sitting up front beside her. I didn't ask her about it that evening at home. I assumed it was a colleague of hers from her new school. I happened to spot the two of them together again on a different occasion. This time the man was driving the car and my wife was seated beside him. Then she started getting calls on her cell phone, which she had acquired early on, possibly to facilitate communication with her new colleague or lover. She wouldn't answer before going out to the front of the building in the shade of the pine tree. She'd go on talking for a long time and come back in silence, preparing the answer to a question I never stooped to ask her even once.

I got together with my hotel friend at one of the city's first-class restaurants. He offered me a fancy cigar and a glass of cognac. He believed that fine clothing and a beautiful locale encouraged two people having a conversation to divulge the best they had. He, by the way, did not think favorably of conversing with more than one person at a time, since with more people involved, the conversation got drowned in routine banalities. We enjoyed a long silence before he told me that the proprietress at Beryt Sur Mer was still perched in her usual spot in the lobby, but the place was losing its flavor and the number of journalists seeking it out was on the decline. He considered it a war hotel. If the current conditions calmed down, the hotel would lose its foreign clientele, who were enamored with wounded cities. He was the only person I could talk to about my marital woes. He said that I was like him, not cut out for marriage, and suggested I figure out a way to escape the mess I'd gotten myself into.

"Life is already an elaborate trap. How much worse if you add marriage to the mix?"

I shared my doubts about my wife's behavior with him. He appeared to have been expecting that and volunteered to surveil her. For a string of days, he observed her from the sidewalk across the street from the school, monitoring her every move. He came back to me with the conclusion that she was in love with a man who accompanied her every day on her way out of the school building. I was relieved when he came back with that. It was a disaster that had the potential to exhume my life from its dark monotony. He advised me again to leave her.

"She'll come to you one day and tell you she's pregnant, and you'll know you haven't touched her for months."

I told him I didn't care about fatherhood and didn't have any feelings of jealousy. I never felt any of that my entire life. Instead, it was as though that man she was meeting on her way out of school every day relieved me of a burden I had no desire to bear. Her unfaithfulness even turned me on sometimes and made me fantasize about sleeping with her. I hadn't realized that I was also to blame for where we'd got ourselves. She was fully confident in her appeal and had hooked up with me, a man who placed her in the realm of the paintings of Greek mythology, but a man who was not aroused by her. Even as a teacher of philosophy who was in the midst of preparing a dissertation on morals and the works of Schopenhauer, my coldness was tantamount to an insult she could not ignore.

Liberated from teaching, I went back to my attempts at writing. Something came into my mind, and my mind alone, as the newlywed—the contours of a character: a young man living on his own on the top floor of the family house. He doesn't open the door to anyone. They send food up to him in a basket. He competes in chess matches against the unbeatable computer program, Deep Blue. He never wins a single round, but never stops, and covers his bedroom walls with drawings of Sisyphus pushing his rock to the top of the mountain before it rolls back down.

I planned for writing but didn't write. All the characters I envisioned were men. Young men, rebels, no girlfriends, no intimate partner, living in voluntary isolation. I could sketch them with the colors of their clothes and their details, but the successive bumps in the road of my life prevented me from giving them the time needed to capture them in the form of Arabic sentences that met my standards for eloquence. My projects remained imaginary drafts postponed to some other time.

I spent hours at the bookstore, reminiscing about my first romance. I'd buy more books, some that were new editions of old publications, until my room was flooded with them. One day, on one of the shelves at "the Arabic Library" I stumbled upon an album of colored aerial photographs of various parts of the country. Mountains and plains. It had been published by the Army's Department of Geographic Services. I flipped through it and landed on a picture of my hometown. There it was in perfect clarity, shot from the sky, its buildings, its river, its orchards, its two churches, and its little streets. I could even easily make out the houses that we'd moved in and out of, and I saw the cemetery where I buried my precious mother. I was struck with a longing and nostalgia I hadn't expected. I still recalled the exuberance I felt when I left the town and the liberating cry I released toward the heavens. My mother's death had helped me make peace with my town, the town no one loves. I bought the book and brought it home.

I decided to confront the situation head-on and put up a fight. I dragged a large table into the empty living room, opened the book to the page featuring our town, and set it on top of the table. I warned my wife not to touch anything. She shrugged without saying a word, turned her back, and walked into her room in a sign of discontent. To get back at her, I decided to construct a scale model of my town. I went over to the hardware store and bought saws, rulers, some wood, cans of paint of all colors, nails of every size, hammers, screwdrivers, adhesives of all types, and I also stumbled upon some little brick molds I could use to craft roof tiles for some of the old, grand houses of the well-to-do. To truly set the project in motion, I also needed miniature figures for pedestrians, cars, tractors, trucks, a cross for the church steeple, and some translucent blue film to represent the river water. I used bags of sand to construct the hill upon which the town is situated, and I attempted to recreate the slow-turning water wheel near one of the cafés that was the town's main tourist attraction. That took me an entire week. I decorated the ground with artificial grass, outlined the river within it, and surrounded it with the orchards owned by people who would never yield an inch of their land no matter the circumstances. They protected those orchards the way they protected their children. I planted them with mulberry and olive trees. I paved the roads and alleys as I knew them. I let my creativity flow as I constructed the old neighborhood where the shops were tightly packed, following the traditional "Baghdadi wall" design which meant adjoining walls between neighboring shops. I proceeded to work on the houses that we moved in and out of. I spent entire days gluing and sawing and measuring, not feeling the time go by. The sun would come up and I'd still be working on the model. I included the high school that had separated the warring factions from each other, and the butcher shop where the owner was killed right in front of his fresh slaughter, and the fabric and buttons shop that the girl with the deep voice like a man used to ogle me from, and my mother's relative's house—the math teacher—who we never heard from after he checked into the mental hospital. I was never able to find that hospital, despite hearing it said that it was in the eastern suburbs. Maybe here somewhere, in the vicinity of our new house. I even devised a method to construct the speaking clock in the church tower, a gift from a town émigré.

I went out one day to visit my father and my aunt, but I didn't find them at home. I sat in the chair where my mother used to sit, waiting for something to happen that might bring me back to her. My aunt came home. She hugged and squeezed me with unexpected enthusiasm. She

135

was the lady of the house now. She begged me to stay for lunch, but a persistent voice was calling me back home. I returned and didn't find my wife there. Instead, I found my town in rubble. She hadn't left a single element the way it was, not a single thing intact. No doubt she had stopped at each piece, smashed it with the hammer or cut it up with the scissors and threw everything that had been set up on the table onto the floor. I imagined that violent and vengeful scene while I waited for her to come home, my cane in hand, gently stroking its handle.

Night fell. I stood in the darkness, ready for combat, unable to sit down or light a lamp. I could hear the hum of car engines and the shouts of the neighbors. Finally, I heard the clicking sound of the key in the door. I straightened up, ready for action. She entered. She switched on the living room light without a word of welcome. She walked past me in her high heels trying not to step on the remnants of the model. I pounced on her, hitting her with all the determination I had within me. She let out a cry of pain like a wounded animal. I dealt her another blow. Her arm was fractured in two places. She fell on her face, crumpled atop all those sharp materials. She was covered in blood.

I called the Red Cross while she lay there writhing in pain. If she said anything at all, it was that I was the worst thing that ever happened to her. I was the archangel of evil, a knight of the apocalypse. I had wrestled her away from her self-imposed isolation from men. I'd seduced her so I could annihilate her. We might have resumed our philosophical discussions at that moment if the paramedics hadn't arrived and rushed her to the hospital, with her wincing in pain every time she moved her hand. I didn't flee anywhere. I stayed at home waiting for the situation to unfold however it may. I sat on the floor with my back against the wall and my head between my hands. There was a knock at the door at the hour when the nightingale in the pine tree pipes his birdsong, waking up the day. An officer from the State Security came in with two deputies. They mentioned they had a search and inquiry warrant issued for me. They handcuffed me and silently escorted me to the military jeep parked outside. I remember that I wasn't disgruntled about what was going to happen to me and that the dawn air was fresh.

MELANCHOLIA

In PRISON, I met with four people who came to see me in succession over the course of two days. The first was the examining magistrate, who sat at the desk and ordered me to keep standing throughout the interrogation. He directed the questions towards me but did not look in my direction. He'd light up another Lucky Strike cigarette as soon as he'd snuffed out its sister in an ashtray filled to the brim. The young men of my town loved those American cigarettes and always had a pack in the pocket of their sheer silk shirts. The poor ones among them got by with buying just three cigarettes, which they lit up, took a few puffs from, and snuffed out several times over the course of the day. All of that was to attract girls, along with a generous amount of Brilliantine to shine their hair. The dialogue with the examiner began politely. He said he knew my town and the difficult nature of its people. He asked if they still followed their custom of taking revenge and spewing harsh curses all the time. He coupled that with a failed attempt to imitate a curse against mothers and the dead that had sexual innuendos.

After a few minutes, he resumed his serious tone and said with a wry nervous smile, "You think the State is powerless and the country is lost. You assure yourself that you committed that crime and the justice system will be the last to know?" As if he was finishing an argument with me that he'd started with some other people. "No, sir," he replied, while I didn't say a word. "The State records things and conceals things, but the State doesn't crumble."

He reached for a gray folder and opened it, keeping his gaze on me rather than examining the papers inside it. It was then that I noticed he was cross-eyed. I wouldn't be able to track where he was looking as he read the papers and glanced at me simultaneously.

"You stand accused of clandestinely exiting the country and enlisting in an armed Palestinian group in the Jordan Valley. There, you managed to penetrate the vicinity of certain Israeli settlements but were subsequently expelled due to your apprehension about engaging with the occupying forces…"

I smiled without correcting him. He continued, "And for your involvement with a banned revolutionary organization in Beirut known as the Arab Trotskyists…"

It was the first time the examining magistrate had ever heard of that gang who'd taken up arms and participated in the civil war. He asked me if Trotsky was an actual person or if he was a figment of our imagination, so I told him we came up with the name because it had a nice ring to it.

He continued reading what was in the file:

"Attempted assassination of a bank owner, and it was revealed in subsequent testimony that you planted the explosive under his car, constituting a clear case of attempted murder. Your logistical involvement in other assassination plots, and now the premeditated attempted murder of your wife."

He concluded his summary with a triumphant note: "The general amnesty granted at the end of the civil war is invalidated for any beneficiary who commits a crime after its issuance. This applies to you." Through me, he was settling all his scores with all the people whom the justice system had failed to apprehend, and there were many of them. He thought he was scaring me, but all he managed to accomplish was to confound me with those cockeyes of his.

The lawyer came the next day. He was neat—wearing the brightly colored tie he never left home without—and the jail cell was filthy. He remained on his feet after lightly touching the chair with his finger and finding a thick layer of dust on it. All through the interview he seemed to be smelling a bad odor that the examining magistrate had left behind with the stink of his cigarette smoke. He was the son of the owner of the shop where my father worked. My father had asked him to represent me. He had on a pair of brown shoes with laces, undoubtedly the finest ones available in his father's shop. He specialized in criminal law. He encouraged me to tell him the truth and said that my secret would remain confidential. I replied that I didn't have any secrets. He said that he had studied my case and it would be possible to plead for an honor crime if we presented witnesses who could testify to the wife's marital infidelity. In fact, the lawyer had heard that my wife had committed that. My witness, who could testify to her infidelity, was ready—the witness to my marriage who would willingly transform into the witness at my trial. The lawyer pulled out the criminal code from his briefcase and proceeded to read to me the articles for reduced penalties for honor crimes. I interrupted him and said that my wife hadn't done anything wrong. I just couldn't stand her being under the same roof with me anymore. We'd disagreed about the choice of furniture for the living room. I preferred leather Chesterfield sofas, and she wanted fabric upholstery, so I hit her. That's all there was to it. In the next meeting with him, he didn't sit. His repugnance toward the place doubled. Our dialogue lasted a few minutes. He stared at me for a while and then asked me if I preferred to stay in prison, even if a chance to be released came along, as though he'd discerned my hidden intentions. So I said "yes."

He concluded by saying, "I can get you out in three months if you cooperate with me."

When I stopped answering his questions, he just shrugged, shut his expensive leather briefcase—the same shade of brown as his shoes—and left, maintaining his immaculate appearance, never to return after terminating his legal representation contract. On his way out, he tossed his written notes about my case in the wastebasket.

My father wasn't long in coming either. He arrived sweating and distressed, with two dark circular stains under his armpits. He was carrying a box of Arabic sweets and a bottle of mineral water that he took little sips from to calm his nerves. I thought he was worked up over the mess I'd got myself into, since the lawyer would have told him about my stubbornness and that the judge might automatically give me the harshest sentence just for not appointing a lawyer. We were catching up with each other. He was asking me what I was going to do, attempting to offer me advice, while I tried to divert him from discussing my case. I asked him about the little African boy. I got the feeling from his hesitation that the boy was a burden to him. My father was talking, but he wasn't there. He wanted to say something and then he'd back away. I kept quiet to give him a chance to speak. Finally, he divulged his secret. It wasn't right for him to be living with my aunt and her son in the same apartment. News would reach the puritanical people of our town, and even the neighbors here in Beirut didn't approve of the idea. As a protective measure, he thought it best for them to get married and he was seeking my approval, adding that this had been my mother's wish before she died. She'd said so to her sister on two separate occasions. He said his peace without stopping, as if he'd practiced delivering this declaration several times beforehand.

He took me by surprise. I felt sad. We sank into a long silence. I looked up at the ceiling and all the cracks that the humidity had caused in the gray paint they used in all government institutions— schools, ministries, prisons. My father concealed his discomfort by endlessly reading the tiny writing on the label stuck to the bottle of mineral water detailing its composition—bicarbonate and calcium and other things. The guard broke the silence and awkwardness when he came in to announce that the visiting hours were over. My father left the room without looking back. We'd become like strangers.

The final visit was from my hotel resident friend from Beryt Sur Mer. He didn't rub it in that he had warned me against jumping into marriage. Instead, he told me he was sick and wouldn't last long. He hadn't told anyone. Not his son in New York, not his wife, whose place of residence he had no idea about. He began experiencing pain in his bones, which, as the doctor had warned him, was likely to intensify. Soon he would start taking pain medication and would live on shots of morphine. He was going to take care of himself. I understood what he meant by "I'll take care of myself," and replied with a nod. I didn't try to change his mind. He had told me his intentions the first time we met. He stood up from his chair and said in a solemn tone, "When you get out of prison, and that will be soon because the sentencing in these kinds of domestic issues is usually light, you'll carry a bouquet of white roses to my grave. Twenty roses, not more, and then you'll go to the hotel where I've left a leather case for you. Here's the key. Take it and say hello to the proprietress. She'll turn up her nose at you as a sign she still harbors passionate feelings for you and remembers your encounters together on the first floor but is trying to maintain some dignity. The final task on my list is selecting a gravesite and covering the expenses. A square meter in the Evangelical cemetery costs more than one of the few lots left zoned for building in the capital. The real estate agents found me a place overlooking the sea with a shy willow tree providing shade over it. We found a statue of a winged angel made of white marble. I visited the place many times and oversaw everything."

My Protestant friend kissed me on the forehead two times. With my eyes closed, I asked him how he planned to carry out the deed. I didn't hear his answer. When I opened my eyes again, he was gone. He left the interview room of the Baabda prison and disappeared from my sight forever.

My father got married secretly in a small church on the northern outskirts of the capital. It was a sad wedding celebration apparently. Just one of his friends attended, someone he'd known since the shoe worker strikes, and my cousin, who told me later on that his mother wore a dark blue dress and my father put on a gray tie. Colors to "break the mourning" over my mother. They asked the priest for assistance in finding a woman from the parish to act as a witness for their marriage contract. He went to search for someone and left them for over an hour sitting silently in the church until he returned with one of the nuns of the sisterhood.

My friend committed suicide. He injected himself with poison and sat waiting for his death while gazing out of his hotel window at the people passing by on crowded Armenia Street. He called out to a friend of his. He'd seen him coming out of one of the restaurants. They exchanged hellos, asked about each other's health, before the poison coursed its way through his blood and had its effect. He fell to the floor—just as they later found him—lay flat on his face and gave up the spirit.

My wife went back to live with her mother after the doctor gave her a three-month renewable medical release from work. She hired a couple of movers to toss all my books into a huge dumpster. She further instructed them to rip up the bulk of my belongings, as though to chop me up and make me disappear. The whore knew that by getting rid of my books in her vengeful act, she was taking down my last defense.

The attorney general requested a five-year sentence, delivering a passionate description of my crime filled with metaphors and excerpts from the epistles of St. Paul concerning marriage, since I was a Christian. Then the judge gave me the opportunity to speak. I thanked the attorney general and the prosecuting attorney and said I didn't have anything to add to their eloquent speeches. The judge looked at me with incredulity. I sensed a tinge of pity in his eyes.

"You hold a degree from one of the best universities in Beirut," he said. "You've taught at its best schools. Surely you can explain the reason for your violent attack on your wife."

I told him how she destroyed my hometown, not leaving a single trace of it intact. I told him that she didn't like leather furniture, didn't want to hang paintings on the wall. We had different tastes in food and colors and what time to go to bed at night. The judge didn't understand what I meant. He sentenced me to just two and a half years.

I had pursued that on my own. In those hours while I waited for my wife to come home, my blood did not cool. In truth, I was intent on committing some crime that would undermine my life. I remembered the cane made of oak that my mother's relative from our hometown—the math teacher—had used to smash the mirrors and break every breakable thing in his house. I quit teaching those teens at the Good Shephard high school the language of Voltaire, having suddenly realized the banality of my work there. My marriage ended as soon as it began. I agreed to the divorce. I signed the papers my wife's lawyer brought to me a month after the incident without reading them. He said that my wife was in very bad shape. She'd had several surgeries. This didn't elicit any feelings of sympathy from me. I signed, but I placed one condition, that she return to me my picture with my aunt and the dog Fox that was hanging in the kitchen of our ill-fated marital home, and the painting of Antar and Abla. The lawyer brought the two pictures a few days later to my parents' apartment, from where I reclaimed them at the end of my prison sentence. The philosophy teacher was out of my life, with her discussions on Schopenhauer's ethics and the enduring impact of Greek philosophy on modern civilization and her tobacco-farming relatives on her mother's side and her small-business owner folks in the city. I found out later that she started wearing chador and joined an Islamic association after relinquishing the study of "secular" philosophy, as she'd started calling it. She was interested in religious studies and started giving lectures on the merits of the Prophet Muhammad and Ahl al-Bayt in a group of "sisters" belonging to the "Good Women Organization," which provided assistance to the mujahideen.

The judge pronounced his sentence, and they transferred me to a nearby prison the same day. Two wide and crowded hallways of cells and two small solitary lockups for disciplining prisoners who conversed loudly back and forth with their prison mates. The first thing the prisoners asked me was what I was in for. They were thrilled to hear about my attempt to murder my wife. They clapped for me and offered their regrets for the bad luck, i.e., failing to kill her. The longtime prisoners caught a whiff of me. They sized me up from my neat attire. One of them, who specialized in stealing cellphones and electronics and was serving his third prison sentence, advised me to hold onto the cash I had in my pockets. Everything here could be bought and sold, from American cigarettes to prison guards. I ate the prison meals, which were difficult to swallow at a time when I had money enough to order food from outside. I didn't buy a new mattress; I inherited one from a former prisoner, which made me itch to the point of bleeding. My father and my aunt were the only two people to request a visit, but I didn't go out to meet them even though the guard kept calling for me. They left me some sweets, which I passed around to those nearby, without even taking a bite. After a second attempt, they quit visiting the prison. The convicts had wives and family members who came to check on them and bring them little presents and cigarettes. The women who lived close would bring their husbands hot meals. Only three of us had no one who looked after them.

The first was a Syrian Kurd who'd woken up one dawn, gathered up all his belongings in the village of Tal al-Dhahab in the al-Hasakah region, and walked off without saying goodbye to anyone in his family. He slept in the rough with the stray dogs. He carried concrete blocks on his back at a construction site at the outskirts of Damascus in return for his daily sustenance. He knew all the poems of Muhammad al-Maghut by heart, although he was afraid to speak them aloud in his homeland, as he said. His final destination was Beirut. The only thing he ever saw of it was a tiny room he rented on the fifth floor, with no elevator, in the neighborhood of Beirut Arab University. He discovered some explosives there that appeared most likely to have been remnants from the arsenal of the PLO, whose main headquarters had been in the area. He turned them over to the security forces and ended up getting arrested and charged with being in possession of them, with no one listening to his story. He was awaiting trial. I spent quite a bit of time with him. Every day he recited Mahmoud Darwish's poem "The Kurd Has Nothing but the Wind," and then they moved him to another place. When we parted I gave him some money. He hugged me and said I was the only beautiful thing he'd encountered since leaving his little town of Tal al-Dhahab in the district of al-Hasakah.

The second was a Lebanese guy who had no one except his mother, who'd gone blind from diabetes. They had been living off the tires and mirrors that he stole from cars in the eastern side of the capital at night and would sell to used-tire and car-part salesmen on the western side the next morning. His mistake had been returning to the same street. He got arrested and received a one-and-a-half-year prison sentence. His mother was left all alone, and she got evicted from her room and ended up sleeping under the stairs. Kind-hearted individuals took pity on her and kept her alive with bread and canned food. She possessed a gold bracelet that she was reserving for her last day. A person sneaked up on her without her noticing, snatched the bracelet off her wrist, and ran off. All of that was according to the prisoner.

And the third one was me.

They summoned me once to go meet with a priest who came to the prison dressed in street clothes and a white collar. The majority of the prisoners were Muslims, but the priest was able to identify the Christians by their names. He asked me if I needed a Bible to keep under my pillow and then started preaching to me, calling me the greatest of the apostles and telling me I should be a role model to the others, a leader to them. He was counting on me to spread the word of God among those pitiable ones with the hope that, despite our small number, we would serve as a positive example to the Muslims.

I didn't like what he was saying, so I decided to provoke him. I told him not to put his faith in me because I'd openly declared my adherence to Islam to everyone in there. I'd recited the two shahadas a week ago and I was going to let my beard grow soon and wear a white robe and sit in the corner contenting myself with nothing but the Quran and the biography of the Prophet. I concocted an extensive lie, which led him to cross me off his list.

They transferred me to other prisons, each with its own smell. The smell of the toilets during the day and the feet of the prisoner lying next to you at night. I got to know all types of convicts. I used to give them packs of cigarettes and lottery tickets, and I paid the administrative fees for some of them to make their final exit to freedom. At night I could feel them sneaking up and picking my pockets. In the morning, I'd look into their eyes and could tell who the guilty party was. I'd smile to his face. They used to write little secrets about their lives on the walls. The names of women and heart-shaped drawings. Wise sayings about the miser and the generous one, Quranic verses and promises to take revenge against unnamed individuals.

They tried to rob me while simultaneously loving me. Their emotions were crude. I talked and listened to them, and they opened up their hearts to me. Those guys, the shabbiest ones, who never went to school a day in their lives, whose hands were rough and fingernails were black from working in car repair shops, whose bodies were tired, seemed to get some rest there in that prison that resembled their lives. They could bear the slow passage of time, unlike some others, men who'd written bad checks and enjoyed having money and leisure at one time or others who'd forged high school diplomas. Those men felt the heaviness of the hours because they had dreams and plans for their lives once they got out of prison.

I didn't complain. After all, I was a semi-voluntary prisoner. Despite that, the melancholia would hit me during the early evening hours. The worst part of the day in prison was at sunset. During recreation time, I would go to the prison yard and walk with a military rhythm, counting my steps as I went out and came back. I'd march, hitting my shoe as hard as I could against the pavement of the courtyard. My head would pound with each step and prevent me from thinking. That way, the period of dusk would pass with the least amount of discomfort. With the fall of darkness, we would go back to the prison hall, which was lit up by a single electric light hanging by a cord from the ceiling. The bulb was filthy, covered with dead flies, and rather than lifting the prisoners' gloominess, its faint light induced deep sadness. One of our prison mates chose precisely that moment every day to start slapping his head with his hands. Then it would escalate into hitting his head against the wall so hard that in the beginning some thought it was a mild earthquake. He'd hit his head while whispering to the Prophet Muhammad and Imam al-Hussein; meanwhile one of his mates would start with a slow, regular moan. That annoyed the prisoners even more than the first guy. It drove them crazy, so they'd start yelling at him to shut up. The prison guards would come and take him out for extra recreation time under the moonlight, in the hope it would calm him down.

Nighttime in the prison was another story. When the room "monitor" turned off the cursed light at ten o'clock, it didn't encourage anyone to sleep. The chatter was constant, and so were the sporadic loud farts they let loose with a variety of rhythms, and the heavy sighs every time one of them turned over in his sleep. There was an Armenian cell-mate near me who tried to get to sleep by endlessly listing all the players on the Homenetmen soccer team, including all the reserve players: Asador, Avedis, Bedros, Garabed, Hovsep, Mardik… until he slipped into his dreams. In the morning, he was merry. He taught me how to make basturma and kebab halabi and told me he worked for the Lebanese Electric Company. Sometimes he climbed up the poles to hang power lines and other times to pilfer them because the copper was worth a lot of money. Some of his workmates squealed on him. He made all sorts of mistakes in Arabic gender agreement as he spoke.

The hot nights were never-ending, and the prison didn't settle down before four am, except when one of them abruptly woke up in terror from a nightmare in which one of his enemies was pushing him to the precipice of a deep well while he tried to resist. Rather than falling, he jolted up, drenched in sweat.

Then, the conflicts erupted on the streets of the capital, as the Sunni and Shiite sects engaged in hostilities, a departure from two decades of strife that had primarily involved confrontations between Christians and Muslims. Gunfire erupted, with no one certain about its origin, and it was soon accompanied by the burning of tires and the blocking of roads. Its repercussions penetrated the prison walls in the form of clashes between the convicts and threats to settle scores when they got out. The Christians took on the role of peacekeepers. One time I stepped in in my capacity as an "educated" person to give a lengthy explanation in which I told the Shiites that the Sunnis revered Ali Bin Abi Talib and al-Hussein, and I pacified the Sunnis that the Shiites were just like them, followers of Allah's Prophet. I told them that in any case the events that had caused their division dated back over 1,400 years. They calmed down for some time, but the big prison hall witnessed a sharp rift whereby the adherents of the two Islamic sects who were thieves, statutory rapists, and drug dealers congregated on opposite sides of the jailhouse, where they continued betting together on horse races and European football matches while their Christian minority counterparts convicted of similar crimes gathered in the middle of the hall. Some of them started calling me "Hajj," while the others weren't fooled by my extensive knowledge of Islamic history. There were two Druze men among us who'd been convicted for the attempted murder of their sister in an honor crime case. Their accent had given them away. They sat off on their own, sipping matte and commiserating over their failure to erase the shame that had chased after their sister, or which she had chased after and willfully brought upon herself, or so they said. They threatened to finish the job as soon as they got out.

The rift exploded with the assassination of the prime minister. A mass scuffle broke out in our hall as soon as the news broke. The two camps became embroiled in a brawl that included hitting each other with water bottles and shoes, and spewing curses attacking Ahl al-Bayt from one side and the Companions of the Prophet—specifically Aisha and Uthman Bin Affan— on the other. The fighting would cool down, and then a word from here or there would be enough to reignite it until one of them pulled out a knife, which no one knew he'd been hiding the whole time. The guards intervened with their weapons, and some of the hot-headed ones from each side were moved to other prisons.

I never met anyone in prison who was innocent or claimed to be innocent. They were proud of their deeds and sometimes even the depravity of those deeds. And I met one for whom prison had become home. He'd do his time, get set free, and immediately steal a motorcycle or molest an Asian domestic worker, something that would land him back where he was—because he was no longer capable of taking care of himself on the outside. He would plead with the judges, who had become his familiar acquaintances, to grant him an extended sentence. They would smile and do what they could to help him out. During my stay among them, I became their letter writer, the same service I used to perform for my neighbors in my hometown as a teenager. I would craft some words of criticism to a daughter who hadn't come a single time to visit her father. The father would talk, weep, and attempt to make his tears drip onto the paper. All the prisoners would congregate around him until a teardrop fell, next to which he'd ask me to write, "This is your father's teardrop, dear daughter." Some of the men would laugh while others got choked up. Or a second prisoner would ask for money from his rich and stingy brother. And a third wrote to his wife. We'd go off to a corner of the jail, just the two of us, because he didn't want the others to hear him threatening her: "If I hear again that you've been flirting with our neighbor the water seller, if he comes near our home, I will kill you the moment I get out of prison."

I toned down the death threat, but I found out later that he killed her after he was set free. He invited her out to a picnic by the riverbank. It was early spring. They had lunch, then he relaxed, puffing on a hookah. In the end he shot her and threw her body in the river.

After that I would write short text messages for them on their smartphones, which came into the prison during the last year of my sentence—a few memorable months when the device helped bring about silence in the prison. The residents would spend their days with their noses pressed to their phone screens playing solitaire to kill time. Then the convicts started having conversations with their relatives and acquaintances, causing the prison to lose its meaning. Visits dwindled, which they made up for with long phone chats that extended into the night: the caller in a hushed voice wooing a girlfriend he hoped would be waiting for him when he got out; and the one who shouted at his partners in a smuggling operation, demanding his cut that they neglected to give him after he ended up in jail. He was the only one who got punished and he'd paid the price for all of them; or a conversation that started out calmly and crescendoed to loud curses.

Eventually, the phones were confiscated and their use was strictly prohibited, even though it was still possible to smuggle them into the prison for a hefty sum, making them the most expensive sort of gift one could receive. The state had no luck in eradicating cell phones from prisons. People who were able to sneak them inside kept them on silent to avoid getting caught, unless they forgot to do so and ended up waking everyone with a loud ring in the middle of the night.

Before the end of my sentence, a quiet young man dressed in a suit and a striking necktie appeared on the other side of the bars. He looked like he'd emerged from one of those American movies about racial discrimination. Next to him was one of the prison wardens. The prisoners started howling at the sight of him for the mere fact of his dark skin. He'd changed. I didn't realize who he was until the warden called me to come out and meet him. An uproar ensued all around me and as I headed in his direction, I was forced to announce that the young man was my maternal cousin. Instead of settling down, on account of my relation to him, the prisoners took it as a reason to howl even louder. With the boy standing right there, they yelled out some loaded innuendos about my aunt, saying surely she had enjoyed herself in bed with whichever black man had knocked her up. That was accompanied by matching gestures. They stopped when they sensed I wasn't taking kindly to their words. It seemed they all believed in some sort of racially based sexual theory—who knows how they got it into their heads—which claimed that it would bring good luck for a man to sleep with a black woman, and it worked the other way around, too, for a white woman who slept with a black man.

We spoke together in fluent French. He was nice. He'd grown up suddenly. He left school because he couldn't take the students' abuse anymore, but he wasn't bitter. He asked how I was doing and then said his home life wasn't happy either and he wished he could move somewhere else. I asked him to wait for me, told him I was getting out soon, and we could look for a house to live in together. I told him I wasn't keen on visiting my parents' house either. He couldn't believe his ears. He said if living with me didn't work out, then he would make preparations to leave for Ivory Coast.

YAMOUSSOUKRO AND TAL AL-DHAHAB

THEY CALLED ME up for early release, three months before the official end of my sentence, for good behavior. The sergeant yelled my name at a volume that didn't really fit the distance separating us. My prison mates bid me a sincere farewell and gave me the same round of applause they'd greeted me with when I first got there.

"Goodbye, Teacher. May you never come back here again!"

I exchanged heartfelt farewell hugs with everyone, fully aware that there was no possibility of reuniting on the outside. I promised the sad young man from the village of Tal al-Dhahab, near al-Hasakah, that I would join up with him when he finished his prison sentence. He mentioned having no idea how long his sentence would be or even why he was being sentenced in the first place. He had no clue when it would end. He hadn't even appeared before the judge yet. When the warden summoned me, I pleaded with him to look into the Kurdish guy's case because he was being treated unfairly. He pursed his lips, handed me my things, and I went on my way. I didn't ask for my cane, but one of the security guards came after me with it.

"The murder weapon! Don't do that kind of thing again. You seem like a nice man."

The first landlord my cousin and I approached didn't invite us in. He was still in his pajamas. His right cheek was covered with shaving cream. We could hear him inside before he opened the door, cursing and making threats. We weren't sure if there was someone else in there he was directing his crass words at. He took a long look at my new partner.

"You want to rent the apartment for him?"

"No, for him and me."

He didn't like the mixing of races, so he put on a show of excuses.

"Someone already came and put down a deposit. Yesterday."

It was obvious he was lying. He slammed the door in our faces before we'd even turned to leave.

A middle-aged woman, with a strange accent and thick black eyeliner, gave us a chance. She wanted to know every detail about us. She asked if I was married. She couldn't believe that my aunt's son was black, and so dark and had the name of the greatest archangel. She assumed it was a nickname. Her seductive glances reminded me of the proprietress at Beryt Sur Mer. She shared with us that she lived alone on the top floor and told us ghosts often opened the windows and came into her room. She thought our presence would be a nice distraction. I grabbed my cousin's hand and got away from there. My energy to satisfy women's desires had run out.

"You didn't like her," my companion said. My answer was ready: "I don't like all of them. I don't have anything to do with women since my mother died."

The third landlord was a man of few words, with a pale face, and didn't ask us a single question. He hastily signed the lease and had a copy ready to hand over after we paid six months' rent in advance. We understood why he'd been so hasty after spending our first night in the apartment, which was adorned with tasteless furniture made of cheap wood and coarse upholstery. The living room walls featured two faded pictures of the temple of Baalbek and the Cedars of God. The place dripped with the gloominess of furnished apartments, where previous tenants leave no trace of their personal tastes or their temperaments, and so what remains behind them is an emptiness that wrings the heart. Right from the very first night, it became clear that the landlord had conned us. The building overlooked the highway, the Beirut exit road in the direction of the Beqaa Valley and Damascus. Day and night, there was no end to the noise of car motors and fuel and cement trucks, which made it impossible to sleep until the crack of dawn even when you were totally exhausted.

My companion found a part-time job at the information desk at his country's embassy. That guy from Yamoussoukro felt comfortable around, even though his mother advised him to keep his distance.

"Yes, he's my sister's son, and he's well-educated, but he has a tendency towards violence. He's the one who got himself into all his problems."

She told him what I'd done to my wife, how I'd nearly killed her, and how I'd refused to receive them—her and my

159

father—when they came to visit me in prison. And she'd heard other strange things about me. "He's challenging to live with, quite exhausting," she remarked.

As for him, he woke up late one morning on one of his days off and, in a quivering voice, suddenly asked me while rubbing his eyes, "Who am I?"

Who was he—good question. He'd caught me off guard. I claimed I didn't understand his question to give myself a little extra time. He told me about a man who used to wait for him at the school gate at the end of the school day in Yamoussoukro. He described him as "a tall black man, very tall. Every time, he would give me a bag of colored candies and marshmallows. He'd put his hand on my head and then disappear around a corner. He never spoke a single word. I think he is my real father."

He also mentioned that his mother used to take out a photo from her purse, showing a white man with a moustache and a stern expression, resembling the men in this area.

"She said he was my father and had died of a heart attack. That's all I know. I was little and didn't question how a black boy like me could come from the marriage of a man and a woman who were white."

After the man with the moustache died, some white men he thought might also be from Lebanon used to visit them at their house. His mother forbade him from sitting with any of them and would send him to his room as soon as they arrived. I was unsure how to evade his question, so I asked him when he was going to turn eighteen.

"In a month."

To which I replied, "I'll tell you in a month."

He accompanied me the next day to the hotel where I'd resided for a long period. We got directions beforehand to the Evangelical cemetery. There are graveyards for all the various religious denominations in Beirut. Seventeen cemeteries. We had to bribe the guard to let us in. He was familiar with all the members of that sect, and we weren't one of them. Plus, he was concerned about theft. He accompanied us to my friend's grave where I placed the white roses. Twenty roses exactly, just as he had requested. The guard left us alone after that. We discovered a wreath of artificial flowers on his grave as well, sent by the young man with the athletic build who used to visit him frequently at Beryt Sur Mer.

We sat in the shade of the willow tree as the sounds of the city died down outside the cemetery. My friend had had a line from T.S. Eliot's "The Wasteland" engraved on the marble plate beneath the winged angel.

> What are the roots that clutch, what branches grow
> Out of this stony rubbish? Son of man,
> You cannot say, or guess, for you know only
> A heap of broken images …

I informed my aunt's son that the man who had passed away was from my father's generation, and if I had to pick between the two, I would choose him. I also told him that many of the people I loved had died, leaving me all alone. We stayed there until sundown. The guard forgot about us or maybe he thought we'd left. He locked the gate and went on his way. We leaped over the fence as if fleeing certain death and walked down adjacent Armenia Street.

The hotel seemed quiet, with no sign of any guests. Not even all the lights were switched on. The hotel owner burst into a loud laugh when I entered the lobby with my cousin. With one sentence she spilled out all her ire: "Your friend," she said, referring to the hotel resident whose grave we'd just come back from visiting, "liked young men. He used to bring them to his room. He really liked you. It looks like you caught the disease just when he died."

When I told her he was the son of my aunt, she snickered at me, certain I was lying.

"Some people like associating with blacks. Where did you fish him out from?"

I felt she was getting hysterical, or wondered if she was going through menopause, so I didn't push the conversation further. We left the hotel. The case he'd left for me was much bigger and heavier than I'd expected, more like a medium-sized suitcase. It was chestnut brown and made of goat hide. We bumped into the husband as we made our way out the front door. He didn't greet us but rather stood there annoyed, watching us until he was sure we'd left the place, never to return.

I opened the case the next day. Inside was a brand new, disassembled sniper rifle, in all its glory, along with a user manual in Russian and English, a silencer, a long-distance scope, many rounds of ammo, an oiling can, a thick notebook with blank white pages—the type that the banks give out to their high-value clients—with a fountain pen and an ink pot, a box of Cuban cigars, three bottles of Bordeaux, and a copy of *Death in Venice*. I slurped down the wine greedily and smoked the cigars while meandering alone or with my cousin through the streets of Beirut. I wrote my name on the notebook and started assembling the rifle. I would put it away and hide it under my bed when 2 o'clock approached and my cousin was due home from work. He would arrive with pre-made meals for lunch, which would last us until we finished our daily dining out at the cafés in the evening. Bohemians par excellence.

One day he came back from work and said, "I turned eighteen today." He sat in front of me waiting for me to say something.

I started the story for him in the town where I was born, with the man who left his family and traveled with a young girl who'd been suffering from boredom and managed to seduce him.

"I think that's the man with the moustache in the picture your mother keeps. He has a daughter from his headstrong first wife. Your sister, or half-sister."

"How could she be my sister?"

"Oh, right. Her father is not your father, and her mother is not your mother either."

"My father?" he asked, raising his voice a little.

"I don't know who your father is. I know her husband is the white man with the moustache, and his first wife is still alive and lives in the town where we were born, cursing our family every day. Your mother doesn't dare show her face in that town to avoid being attacked with curses. Your mother got pregnant with you and out you came, with black skin. Not white, not mulatto. I find you more beautiful than the young white men here with their big noses and hair that tends to fall out at an early age. They're a mixture of ancient Semitic peoples. Phoenicians, Turks, Kurds. Mediterranean people who lived near the ports and Syriacs of square build, and Arabs, too, of course, pure-blooded and olive-skinned. And they say Crusaders and Circassians with blue or green eyes. Little remnants from numerous peoples and races. The end result is not ideal."

The map got complicated, so we sank into silence. After a little while, he said, "I'll be going back to Yamoussoukro soon. The tall black man once gave me an African amulet. A piece of ebony wood with his name and address engraved on it. I kept it hidden from my mother. I'm going to go look for him. My land is there. I dream of riding with him on the back of an elephant or walking barefoot leading a giraffe. I won't be coming back to Beirut. Beirut doesn't want me."

He went to work at the embassy. I finished assembling the rifle and waited. I decided to do things out in the open during the day, because the dark of night might reveal the flame of the gunfire and make it possible to determine where the shots were coming from. I spent several days taking the rifle out and setting it up in the window at the back of the balcony where it couldn't be seen from anywhere except the distant highway. I'd hide the barrel of the rifle in a bushy green plant growing in a pot. Total camouflage. I'd aim at the windows of buildings in front of me and at passing cars. Sitting within my rifle sights, I could clearly see the drivers' heads and the passengers and the residents inside the nearby buildings drinking coffee on their balconies. A married couple who spent most of the day on their balcony, eating, receiving visitors, playing cards, and hanging out at night. I would take one shot, once on Tuesday, the next time on Friday. Usually, the cars would slow down due to traffic, making it easier to aim, but I preferred to shoot at moving targets. If they got hit, they'd keep going a little, moving away from the place where they'd been shot, and that made it difficult to determine where the bullet had been fired from.

During that time, I received some news about my father. He'd reached retirement age and was still working nonetheless, but he'd started openly harassing women. He'd help them try on shoes and caress their feet while saying things with a wink and a nod. When the owner of the shoe store received a second complaint against my father, he fired him. Even though he was in good health, he was out of work, had no friends and no social engagements.

My aunt was getting bored. She'd been seen wandering around the neighborhood near the house. Sometimes she'd forget to make lunch, so my father would scold her and raise his voice at her. If she was late getting home, he would go out looking for her. Once he found her telling her life story to a shop owner. He grabbed her by the arm and dragged her up to the apartment.

About my former wife, I'd heard that she abandoned her religious regression and went back to studying secular philosophy. She abruptly traveled to Berlin to finish her dissertation on Schopenhauer and got married there to a divorced German man with two children. She frequented bars with him and drank beer after letting her hair and her shoulders loose, and she changed her last name to his. Many German scholars admired this Arab woman who was proficient in their philosophy. She had persisted in her effort to learn the language of Goethe. Her parents disowned her and cut her out of the inheritance.

My Kurdish friend got released from prison. The judge declared him innocent of all charges, with the exception of entering the country illegally. The judge scolded the attorney general, saying, "Why did you put this man in prison? He came to you of his own volition to turn over explosives. I am setting him free."

He pounded his wooden gavel, declaring the case closed. I bumped into my friend by chance. There he was, gazing at the high-story buildings and the shiny storefronts with their fancy clothes on display. He gave me a big hug, and then I brought him to live with us after he told me that he was homeless and had nowhere to spend the night. I lived some beautiful days during that time. The African spoke French and the local Dyula language of Ivory Coast, the Kurd spoke very good Arabic, possibly better than his native tongue, and I spoke three languages—Arabic, French, and English. A miniature Tower of Babel. I usually waited for the apartment to be empty—a little before noon, when one went to work and the other wandered aimlessly in the streets—to take out the rifle, feel it in my hands, and take a practice shot into the air.

In the afternoon we'd go downtown or to Hamra Street, have a beer and some spicy Armenian sandwiches. We'd go into the cinema and come back out if we felt the movie was boring. We'd loiter until late into the night. The Kurd would tell us how their native language was forbidden in school, and they only spoke it at home. Every morning they were forced to sing the praises of the president and his young son after him. They lived in extreme poverty. They planted wheat and sometimes ate nothing but dry bread. The six members of his family slept in the house's one and only room. Half of them slept up on the roof in the hot months. One day he was told that someone found a Syrian lira on the ground, so all the children of the town walked with their necks bent down hoping to make a similar discovery. Contrary to his siblings and cohorts, he loved school and took sides with the administration against troublemakers when the administration threatened to close the school if the young Kurdish kids didn't do their homework and accept being disciplined. He made it to the secondary school level with ease and began reading literary books and poetry collections. He harbored a strong desire to run away that he didn't tell anyone about. He felt he'd acquired the qualifications to confront the city. A teacher who belonged to the prohibited Communist Party encouraged him to go.

"What have you got to do with the wretched folk here? Go. Open your wings and fly."

He only left a note for his mother, asking her not to be sad about his departure because he was forging a new path for himself in this dismal world.

"The Kurds are damned," he would say at the conclusion of each chapter of that wretched saga.

I fired my first shot at an older-model green Mercedes that was serving as a taxi. I aimed at the front end. I could have hit the driver in the head but ended up just shattering the rear windshield. After all, the target was moving, and the shooter was a beginner. The driver, an older gentleman, pulled the car over to the side of the road and got out to investigate what happened. He looked in every direction. He stood for a long time in front of the shattered window. He thought maybe a rock had flown up from beneath the tire of one of the cars speeding past him and hit the window. He lit a cigarette while looking all around all over again. He didn't see anything but the speeding cars and the silent buildings. He started the motor, which made a popping crescendo, and the Mercedes disappeared around the first corner. The shattered glass continued to sparkle beneath the brilliant sun.

My cousin returned from the embassy very happy. I saw his bright white teeth for the first time.

"I found out who my father is," he told me. "And I'm close to finding out where he is. The ambassador helped me. It appears he'd been a supporter of the defeated Koudou Gbagbo Laurent. He'd been one of his well-known leaders. The ambassador had no difficulty figuring out who he was, because his name had appeared often in the media and in the civil war, and diamond smuggling to neighboring countries. We just need to track down exactly where he lives, because he's in a constant struggle with adversaries aligned with Alassane Ouattara. Now I know why he used to come secretly to my school. He didn't want anyone to recognize him. I'm leaving soon no matter how much it costs to try to find him."

"But he won't recognize you," I cautioned him, "and your mother doesn't acknowledge his existence."

"He will know me. Fathers have instincts, too. At any rate, I've already bought a ticket and am not going to change my mind."

My next two shots landed in an open space way off their targets. On Tuesday, I had aimed at an Audi. Black, newer model, the kind the nouveau riche boast about owning. And on Friday, I shot a bullet at a Pepsi-Cola truck. I might have shattered a bottle or two, but no one noticed. I stuck to my schedule and didn't get too excited about hitting my targets. On the fourth try, I put a hole in the front tire of a four-wheel drive vehicle, causing it to go off course. It swerved right and left, almost hit the guard rail, and would have flipped down the slope if the driver hadn't managed at the last second to get it under control and bring it to a stop. He got out of the car, terror on his face, and started talking on his cell phone. He waited for roadside service to come to change the tire for him because he was the well-dressed type, and it would be unimaginable for him to do such a job himself without getting dirty.

My cousin left. I found out the details of his adventure from his mother, who hunted me down as if I were responsible for what happened to him. She told me that he made it to the African capital, went to the address engraved on the piece of ebony, but didn't find his long-cherished wish. All he got was some hateful stares from the people living at that house. But he didn't back off. He went around asking everyone he ran into about the man he thought was his father. He drew the attention of some of the staff at the hotel where he was staying, and one day when he was leaving for the city three men came and kidnapped him at gunpoint. They shoved him inside a car with dark windows that had been parked outside and sped off with him. She figured he must have told them his story, just as he told everyone else, so they decided to send a letter to the man he thought was his father saying they had taken something dear to his heart. It seems the man took stock of his valuables and didn't find anything missing. It never occurred to him that the intended item was the son of the Lebanese woman he'd had a fleeting affair with, who he'd heard had gone back to Lebanon for good, with her son. He didn't respond. Even when they hit the ball back in his court and told him they wouldn't turn over his son unless he paid them a hefty sum, he didn't budge.

"His fate is still unknown," my aunt said. She was going to go look for him. She called me to tell me that and to beg me to look after my father, who would be left all alone. I gave some sort of vague answer and made a doubtful promise.

I still had my friend from Syria, but he would soon vanish, too. He explained how some individuals from the Kurdistan Workers' Party had sought him out in Beirut, offering a substantial monthly salary in exchange for his enlistment. They wanted him to return to northern Syria and engage in combat along the Turkish border. They high-lighted six months of intensive weapons training, equity between men and women, and a communist system that applies to all possessions. He refused. He told them he had other options in life.

"Your party is going to lose the battle, because those who are aligned with it today are going to flip tomorrow."

He asked me for help but refused to tell me what his plans were, knowing that I wouldn't like what he had in mind. I told him to do whatever he wished and gave him twice the sum he'd asked for. He promised to pay me back one day, so I told him to forget it because I didn't need the money. He said goodbye and gave me the phone number of someone who could let me know his whereabouts if we lost touch. And indeed, we did lose touch. I called the number and a Kurdish guy answered. He said he had been expecting my call and we agreed to meet up the next day at a café. They bore a strong resemblance even though they were not related. He was sad. His friend had told him about me, said I was a generous and extraordinary man he would never forget. Recalling him brought tears to his eyes so he stopped talking. He wiped his tears on his sleeve, and before he finished telling the story, I understood that my Kurdish friend was dead. He, too, was dead.

"He wanted the money you gave him to pay his way to Sicily. There was a boat owner who arranged transportation for migrants desiring to leave. He told them they just had to make it to Sicily, and the moment they set foot on dry land the Italian government would take care of them and help them get to Germany and England where there were more job opportunities than in any other country. The second the boat left the shore, the owner—who was in constant fear that his customers would drown and he'd be taken to court—disappeared.

Our friend didn't know how to swim. There were no beaches in his homeland. None of the Kurdish lands had a view of the sea, stuck between countries that didn't know compassion. His compatriot tried to convince him to change his mind, but he had such a longing in his heart to go abroad. He had a desire to discover the far reaches of the world. Halfway there, the boat went off course, was struck by a wave, and capsized. The rescue boats tried to extend a helping hand to the wretched migrants, starting with the children and women. Ten men drowned, our friend among them. He was now at the bottom of the sea. No one tried to retrieve his body. He ended up as fodder for the fish. We said goodbye without leaving a line of communication between us. No phone number, no address. I no longer wanted friends in my life.

I woke up early and set up the rifle in its usual position. I chose incendiary cartridges with a red circle on their base that could ignite a fire wherever they landed. Employees were driving their cars to work. Taxi drivers were hunting for passengers. The number of women behind the wheel was on the rise. One of the drivers had a hole in the tailpipe of his American car and it was bellowing smoke and polluting the air every time he stepped on the accelerator. He was passing ahead of the long line of cars, disappearing from my sights before I could take aim at him. Then the vehicle I'd been waiting for arrived. A slow-moving fuel tanker, an easy target. The driver was using his brakes the whole way. If it was diesel that he was carrying, nothing much would happen. But if it was gasoline, then most likely it would go up in flames or cause a colossal explosion. It'd be a huge disaster. I shot one bullet at the yellow tank and followed up with another shot at the big tire, breaking the rules I'd established. What happened as a result exceeded all my expectations. A flame instantly ignited in the tank of gasoline and in his confusion, the driver swerved toward the middle of the road. He jumped out of his seat behind the steering wheel. I saw him gallop away, fleeing from the impending explosion of his tanker. I could see he was wearing a uniform with the petroleum company's logo on it.

That burning obstacle in the middle of the road surprised the other drivers. The passing cars were unable to hit their brakes fast enough and there was a pile up of more than ten cars that slammed into each other in an unprecedented crash. In less than a minute, the highway leading to the Beqaa Valley turned into a plaza of debris with a widening circle of fire. The entire tanker went up in flames. The firetrucks with their sirens swarmed in and started taking the injured away on stretchers. The sound of a huge crash was heard at the same time. A speeding truck carrying a load of lumber became part of the collision and planks of wood went flying everywhere. The police rerouted the traffic, and a news report came on a few hours later. "A massacre of cars and dangerous conditions on the Beqaa highway."

I stopped watching the news report of the accident. I carefully disassembled the rifle and put it back in its case. I packed up my clothes and left the cursed apartment after returning the keys to the pale-faced landlord. I would not live in the city nor in its populated suburbs. I was the prince of darkness. The inconsolable widower. I would head far away, to the east.

THE CAT AND THE PIGEON

I HADN'T REACHED forty yet—I was thirty-nine and a few months, with some white creeping its way into my hairline, early graying I inherited from my father—when I stood in front of the mirror in one of those hotel rooms one day and started talking to myself out loud, giving myself advice.

"That's enough. The world has run its course with you. Whatever else will happen to you beyond this point will merely be a repeat of what already happened before. You played your music. Now it's time to quietly bow out."

When the sea swallowed up my young Kurdish friend, who'd believed that crossing the Mediterranean and making it to one of the Greek islands or to the shores of Italy would be his life's dream, I got out my journal and wrote down the steps I needed to take to achieve the isolation I desired. I changed my whole agenda. Revenge was no longer an option. The only thing was to be rescued from this ruin.

I began by liquidating the joint bank account I shared with my paternal aunt. I kept the cash at home, put it under my pillow. Stacks of American dollars, just as my aunt had advised years earlier. That had been her last bit of useful advice because the Lebanese lira ended up plummeting in value exactly as she had predicted all those decades ago. And so, those abundant dollars of hers saved me the trouble of having to work. At the bank they called me in to speak with the manager, who looked shocked by this decision of mine and argued that I would be foregoing a substantial amount of potential interest, a number he calculated on the adding machine that was always within reach. He gave up trying to convince me when he saw that my face showed no reaction. He realized he was talking to himself while I looked out the window behind him at the goings-on out in the street.

I went to the grocer in the village I'd chosen for my new residence. He sold everything under the sun, from cherries to local apricots, canned goods, hardware, goat milk yogurt. He even slaughtered a sheep himself every Saturday, transforming into a weekend butcher, and kept a little notebook with a running tab for customers who couldn't pay up until the end of the month. I introduced myself and told him I would be moving into the neighborhood. He was a sweet old man with a white moustache and was quick to tell me about his two sons who had gone to Europe where they were now working. He looked over my shopping list—grains, vegetables, a variety of cheeses, cleaning supplies, and other things—and assured me that he had everything in stock. He mentioned he'd send a delivery boy who would ring the doorbell twice to signal me before leaving the bags of groceries at the front door and going on his way. I paid him in advance. He tried to object but I insisted in accordance with my plan. I paid him in dollars, which made his face light up with satisfaction and made him even more attentive to me.

I tossed my cell phone out the window of my newfound house, which overlooked a valley so deep I didn't even hear it land. At any rate, ever since I'd bought it, entire days would go by without hearing it ring. No one ever called me. I'd only given my number to very few people, and there weren't more than ten names in my list of contacts. The truth is, pretty much my sole interlocuter had been my hotel friend, who was now lying in the Evangelical cemetery. I left the radio behind at my last apartment where I'd lived with my two friends—my African cousin and the other guy, the displaced Kurd. They followed the news on their cell phones (each one on his own phone), so the radio had been reduced to a useless decoration.

I didn't own a television and didn't tell anyone my new address. There wasn't really anyone to tell except my father and my aunt—if she were to come back again from Ivory Coast, where she'd gone to look for her son. So far, she hadn't returned. I believed all news of her son was now lost. Taking hostages for ransom is a lucrative and dangerous business on the Ivory Coast. And the last time I ran into my father on a side street near his home, he planted a big kiss on my forehead to express his delight at seeing me. He claimed he had been looking for me and wanted to know if I was doing OK. But then, as usual, there was nothing more for us to say to each other, so we stood there in silence watching the passersby until he came out with the news that he'd decided to join my aunt in Africa. She'd already rented a house for them there. He was getting ready for his trip and asked me, sort of by the way, if I wanted to move into the apartment since he was getting ready to move out. His moving out was a sign that his journey to Yamoussoukro was going to be an extended one. After my sudden departure from my last house—on the heels of the destruction I caused with the sniper rifle—and my migration to another place of refuge, I didn't try to find out what the consequences of my actions were. I cut myself off from listening to the news and buying newspapers, and I stopped frequenting coffee shops. I wandered aimlessly a bit and then checked into a little hotel called Writers' Inn. I was attracted by the name, which belied the shabbiness of its furnishings, the lack of taste in the choice of colors for the curtains, and the horrible morning breakfast one could barely swallow. I spent two weeks at that hotel, reminiscing about my time at Beryt Sur Mer and the proprietress there and comparing her with the young man with the thick glasses manning the reception desk here, who, forgetting the guests' faces, would ask their names again every morning. Most of the guests were small-business owners or Syrian laborers. The hotel had been given the name Writers' Inn as a joke.

I would head out early, spend my day riding around in taxis, looking for a secluded place to rent, and wouldn't come back until nightfall. My quest led me out of the city and up to a mountain village where I found exactly what I was looking for: one big room sectioned off into a kitchen and a bathroom. A bay window overlooked the city from a height of 700 meters above sea level, providing a view of Beirut draped in smog at all hours of the day from the constant burning of trash heaps into the open air over the seashore and the spewing of carbon emissions from the tailpipes of all the cars—a gray cloud mixed with the colors of the sea in a gradual progression that stretched far to the azure horizon. The landlord expounded on the house's merits as we toured through it. I wasn't responsive to him despite my silent joy at having reached my destination, so he rested his case. I put down a full year's rent and chose the comfortable seat I would sit in every day: a roomy leather couch, very close to the kind I had been dreaming of for our marital home and which my wife wouldn't hear of. The landlord said the owners had left it behind, the same way the previous tenants at our apartment on Makhoul Street had left us the Yamaha piano.

I sit here dressed in an expensive black satin abaya that I bought when I was planning the minute details of this isolation of mine. I get up in the morning, hone my laundering and ironing skills, shave with extreme precision and care, bathe, and fix my hair before getting dressed up nicely, as if heading out to meet someone at a nearby café. I keep my shoes on throughout the day and wear my suit jacket. Some days I even put on a tie. I found a *papillon* tie among my belongings that I didn't hesitate to adorn my dress shirt with on Sundays back when I was still conscious of the sequence of weekdays. And I stand in front of the mirror, making sure I'm satisfied with my appearance and my choices, and then I throw on my abaya and sit. I read here on this couch, eat here, sleep here at night, and lie down here in the afternoon. Little dreams come to me during naps but not during the long sleep. I sit and ask myself if I am really here.

"Who am I?" Just as my teenage cousin asked me one day.

Am I carrying the heavy burden of my birth, or am I merely an invention of my books and my readings? Am I softhearted or a simpleton? Someone whose heart aches at the sight of an intimate scene that no one else even notices? Or am I stone-cold, unable to back away from harm? Where does this cruel façade come from, when I feel deep in my soul that I am vulnerable, affectionate, and captive to the compassion of others towards me? Both dwell inside—a relentless devil and an affectionate brother that can be counted on.

On the topic of books, I was worried in my newfangled solitude about the void, about going down the path to madness, about facing a confrontation in which I would be unarmed without words. So I went to the bookshop I normally stock up from, one last time before barricading myself inside this house, and I spent half a day among the shelves recreating my exemplary library. Twenty books, not more, to protect me and accompany me, that I can bury my head in whenever the challenges become difficult. Current affairs have disappeared from my life, even if they occur out there, because I've lost my ability to connect with them after cutting off all ties with the outside world. I wake up to the sound of an excavator or a power saw at a construction site in the background that I can't see. The sky is blue and the sun is shining, even though we are in the middle of winter, and the sycamore tree, whose tip peeks up at me as it sways in the gentle breeze, has started to lose the last of its golden leaves. I stand near the front window. The city is still there in its smog. I considered buying binoculars but changed my mind because how could I, someone who is intentionally withdrawing from the world, suddenly bring it closer to my eyes?

I pause to prepare a small breakfast for myself, intending to cut down on the size of my meals, because I read that the body can sustain itself on very little. Silence settles outside and is only pierced by the din of a military helicopter that hovers nearby and then recedes into the distance.

One day, around noon, I detect some movement behind the curtain of the window across from my room, shadows swaying. I say *around* noon because when I first moved in here, I got rid of an expensive Patek Philippe watch my ex-wife had given me as a gift that I'd forgotten to remove from my wrist. I say I got rid of it, but in reality, I took a hammer I found in a drawer and smashed it, as an act of vengeance for the crime that my wife, the philosophy teacher, committed against the replica of my hometown and my books. From where I sit cross-legged all hours of the day and night, I can see a wall of chiseled stone with a window cut into it and a red tiled dormer over it. The wood of the window frame is red, and its sheer curtain is white. There's just a small aperture for me to look through from where I sit. A little triangle I can peer through each day to see the color of the sky and predict whether it will be clear or rainy. The window has remained shut since I moved in here and no one has ever appeared in it. No shadow, no spirit, as though the owners of the house emigrated to some other country. But just now I sensed some movement there. I'm not sure if someone has come home or if what I saw was a reflection in the window of something that moved outside. I don't like the idea of having a new neighbor. I'm afraid the tenants' return home will muddy this tranquility I've been enjoying. Since their window is adjacent to my room, they could easily infiltrate my intimate circle with one glance.

The one movement I observe daily belongs to a flock of pigeons. Multicolored pigeons from the city and the public squares. Reddish green heads and feathers of various gradations of gray culminating in a black tail. A group of more than twenty birds that have made the red tiled roof across from me a rest stop for themselves. I tried counting them, and I discovered that sometimes there are even more due to the efforts of what is called the "julep pigeon," which lures in birds from other winged flocks. The pigeons take off all at once. They flap their wings and fly away. And I wait until fatigue brings them back to their refuge. The process continues throughout the day until the sun starts to set. The pigeons meet up in one long line, incline their fragile little heads, and go to sleep. Their comings and goings divide the day, and their final return home in the evening is an indication that night has begun. They move in unison, perhaps by means of a secret signal from the leader of the flock that I have been unable to detect or figure out. All I know is that takeoff always happens the moment I'm not expecting it, without any movement or cooing sound in advance.

And then, out of nowhere, perched on the edge of the roof, is a scruffy, appearing more untamed than domesticated. An alley cat. He approaches the flock of resting pigeons and, with such alacrity that the group hasn't the slightest chance to fly away, he clamps his mouth onto the neck of one of them, the last one on the right at the end of the tightly packed row. He takes off with her as the others take flight to save themselves. I leap up from my couch. I open the window to scream at the cat to scare him off, but he has already captured his victim and snuck away, back to his hideout. I feel so discouraged over losing one of my friends that I keep a vigilant watch for the wily tomcat. I will not let him do it again.

After that, I turn to my own self and start stripping it of all its defenses. I choose one of the twenty books that I have, reading it slowly over the course of a few days and then going back to it once more before bidding it farewell. It takes me about a week to ten days to finish a book before tossing it into the fireplace. I contemplate the way James Joyce's *Dubliners* burns as I tear the pages out one by one and feed them to the fire, slowly, entertained by their transformation to ashes and smoke. Everything I am doing is meant as a challenge to my *self*, stripping away every form of intrusion to test its resilience. I go on reading and burning. *Pedro Paramo* by Juan Rulfo, *Journey to the End of the Night* by Ferdinand Céline, which takes half a day to burn, al-Nuffari's book *Al-Mawaqif wa al-mukhātabāt* (*Attitudes and Correspondences*). Each book has a distinct, repugnant odor linked to the quality of its paper and ink. All those luminous characters, comical and tragic, are melting away, but I am not going to back down until my entire arsenal is depleted. I always yearned for books, held onto them dearly, and yet here I am, tossing them into the fire. Man, as they say, is a deep dark well.

The final book I dispose of bears the title *Illuminations*. It was a small record of chaotic emotions, a work attempting to refashion the world from its own fractured pieces. This was the creation of a young Frenchman, not even twenty at the time, who subsequently sought to distance himself from this creation, delving into drug use and engaging in the weapons trade between the port of Aden and some cities in Ethiopia. As though he had abruptly reverted to a more conventional sense of maturity, he said that what he had written there was nothing but a series of meaningless musings of no importance whatsoever. Nevertheless, his sister, who believed in his genius, kept some copies that were reprinted and published all over the world in all languages. After finishing *Illuminations*, I don't throw it away immediately. I keep it in my pocket for a few days as ammunition. I repeat excerpts from it out loud while pacing the floor of my room lengthwise and cross-wise, trying to dance without rhythm before succumbing to the idea of liberating my self from it. And so, I set it on fire in the hearth, and for reasons I don't understand but possibly due to the timely gust of wind outside, or some flaw in the chimney's design, the smoke from *Illuminations* is forced back into the room, engulfing it and making me feel queasy. I would have suffocated if I hadn't rushed to open the windows and stand next to one, breathing in cold air from outside while frantically waving my arms to expel the smoke out the window. And in an instant, I find myself with nothing left to read, devoid of the words of others. I've been condemned to listening solely to my own voice, a voice unnourished by the pens and fiery emotions of brilliant writers, left with nothing but my own nearly exhausted self.

With the onset of the harsh winter season in the mountain village, the pain in my leg has returned—the same leg that was fractured when militiamen fired upon me at the crossing that divided the two Beiruts many years ago. It has come back in the form of successive bouts of pain that sometimes wake me up at night, stop suddenly, and then revisit me without cause when I'm not expecting it. It's as though the pain is always there but has been stifled by the noise of the world and now, due to the quiet that inundates my days, I've started to feel it. The pain reaches a climax, and I can't help but let out screams. I will not ask for painkillers. I will not go out to the pharmacy. I will struggle against the pain on my own, with my will and my patience. I can almost take pleasure in it when it escalates and engulfs all other emotions.

The butterfly imprisoned with me in the room … beautiful, blue with black spots … I've opened the windows for her several times so she can find a way to escape, but she never does. She keeps fluttering about the house instead. She lands on Abjar's tail (in the painting of Antar riding on his horse), or on my face in the picture that depicts me with my aunt, the dog Fox, and General De Gaulle, which I hung on the wall in front of the couch where I spend most of my day. This lovely butterfly brings me back to my hometown and my childhood. She transports me to that age when everything leaves an indelible mark, when perhaps everything takes shape. She also brings me to the places that I've perpetually carried with me in my literary imaginings. Most of the scenes I lingered over in my storytelling unfolded on the riverbank, in the vicinity of the church, or within the quarter surrounding the houses we lived in. In the same way, I now find myself pausing and reflecting once more, fixating on the expression in my aunt's eyes. I can't recall how I felt when the photographer directed us in his customary manner before the flash illuminated our faces. I forget the butterfly. She disappears for days among the things in the house and then suddenly reappears. She's

185

also puttering around near me and near the lantern in her constant effort to have a reunion with the light.

In addition to the picture, I also kept the rifle. It gave me a sense of invincibility and control. A last line of defense. But I was quick to dispose of the bullets, to ward off the idea of killing myself, or of choosing some targets in the area to shoot at from my window again. I settled for assembling the rifle, oiling it, and bringing the scope to my eye. Then I'd take it apart again and put it back together once more until I finally got bored with it.

One evening, while observing the movements of the pigeons as they came home to the red-tiled roof, I came to the realization that I was gradually turning into the solitary characters I had once envisioned and then discarded. Undoubtedly, I, much like those characters whose fates intrigued me, bore some indescribably inherent affliction. It delighted me to think that defiance coursed through my veins, and I was unable to mend my self. If fate had an eye, I was eager to confront it, like we used to do as neighborhood kids to challenge each other. Whoever blinks first loses the duel.

The days recur, one just like the other, until they sink into the fog. I've lost track of the dates and the days of the week. The bells of the nearby church are my only guide for Sundays or holidays when they ring at odd times. When they start broadcasting hymns from loudspeakers, I realize that Christmas is near, whereas Holy Friday hymns like "The Bereaved Mother," which I used to swoon to in my childhood, alert me that it's almost Easter. I am swimming in a fog that has no shape and no structure. I tremble when a knock comes at the door with no warning, before I remember the young delivery boy who brings me groceries and whom I've never seen. One time my heart starts beating fast when there is a knock at the door that has a different rhythm. It keeps coming incessantly. I stop short of shouting that no one is home. The hard knocking on the door won't stop. It is dusk. I lie back on my couch and pull the blankets over myself. The knocking keeps coming. The world is calling me. I hear a voice at the door, "Who's in there? It's the mayor."

"What do you want?" I say, trembling.

"Just making sure you're OK. No one has seen you since you arrived. We thought maybe you paid the rent and didn't move in, until the storeowner told us that he's been supplying you with food and other things."

"Thank you. I'm fine."

"Are you sure everything is OK? If you need anything don't hesitate to call me." He tells me his cell phone number, which I don't write down.

I hear him say to whoever is with him, as they walk away, "The man is unhinged. He'd be better off locking himself up in one of the monasteries."

The truth is that, to me, the more I am alone, the more pleasurable it is. From time to time and for short periods, a wave of enthusiasm that I don't understand creeps over me and sends me dancing in the middle of the room. I spin around to no rhythm, humming jubilantly, with my arms spread out like a swan getting ready to fly, even though a bout of excruciating pain in my injured leg ensues. As evening starts to fall, I stand by the window. My shadow stretches far into the distance in the direction of the city while I recite "The Circassian War Song" or "The Death of the Eagle," poems whose memory had been erased, along with the poets who composed them, but which I still know by heart in every detail from my schooldays.

I still have one of my little treasures left, the letters that I wrote during a bygone summer to a woman who was seduced by words more than anything else. I take them out and read them aloud slowly. I kiss each one and then make it into a paper airplane, open the window, and send it flying on the wind and plunging into the little valley below the house. I become enthralled with the world just as it is, celebrate it for no reason, without actually experiencing anything that would make a person happy, and then I break. Like a swing carrying me high up and then hurling me back down. My voice cracks as I cry out. I scream at the sky or resume the habit from my adolescence formed in our house that the mortar shells got to in the end—I pull the blankets over my head, pour out my sorrows, and cry for my mother to come and save me.

Light and darkness cascade over me in succession. Clear skies and rain. Sleep is mixed with waking. Life has lost its order and I've started forgetting words and the names of things, though I persist in trying to remember them. When I retrieve the past, many of the details are gone from my memory. Faces come to me, and scenes I never really cared about at the time. The connections between our numerous houses have all been severed in my mind, and I can't remember the reason we moved to Beirut or the places in its various neighborhoods where we lived. I am unable to revive the emotions that provoked me to beat up my wife or that made me lash out against rich people despite never living poor myself. My ravenous desire for women has been obliterated. Nothing remains of it but the echo of sexual urges. I remember the women who loved me, but I forget their names. Nothing emerges from that fog but faces and momentary flashes, like when that young woman told me at sunset in that village where we spent a rare summer, "My soul is dead, my friend. Your kisses and your words bring it back to life."

I am immersed in one of these moments when I feel a trembling like an earthquake. A tumultuous wave emanating from the belly of the earth rises up from the city all the way to the mountain where I am living. Everything in the house shakes. Nearly all the glass around me shatters. I get up and go to the window and see what looks like an enormous mushroom over the city. The explosion is massive, a column ascending into the sky. A progression of colors. Thick. White and black and brown and yellow-orange. A concoction of poisons that make the city seem like it is spewing everything in its guts out into the air. I stare at this strange cloud for a long time. Eventually I open the window and in comes a smell that burns the heart, and from outside I hear a long, intermittent scream. I can't understand what is being said, but the cry of distress overpowers all other sounds.

Death falls on the city, and the pigeons don't come home to roost on the red-tiled roof today. They fled to another refuge and will return in a few days. Only the spirit of evil appears—the filthy wild tomcat with his graceful gait and his scruffy black fur, hunting his prey. He slinks to the edge of the roof and, for the first time, disappears in the direction across from where he appeared. The butterfly continues to

189

flitter between the window and the closet and the lamp in a feverish movement until she too finds an escape route and disappears for good. I go back to my seat. I am not about to breach my isolation to find out what happened off at some distant city port. That fate was written for it, and I have no power to change anything about it. I put my head in my hands and get lost in thought for hours in which I imagine that my mother passed down her fear of aging to me, a big baby who keeps trying to get off a train. He calls out in distress and there's no one there to answer. I imagine my mother and don't see her, but the moment I open my eyes and raise my head from under the covers, my paternal aunt appears before me in the picture that brought us together along with the incomprehensible and everlasting panic in her eyes. That traveling photographer, who announced himself by clicking his flash successively while standing at the door, had managed in one random shot to capture in my aunt's gaze the culmination of my life. Now, and after time has run its full course, the men will come knocking at my door. Some will be in military garb and some in sherwal and shirt, with rifles on their shoulders. They will come at the peep of dawn, and I will be asleep. I will wake up, and I won't answer the door, and I won't shout, "Who's there?"

They will go to extremes pounding on the door and employing sharp tools, and in the end, they will manage to break the door open. They'll come inside. They'll search everywhere, trying to find in which place, the kitchen or the bathroom, I might be hiding from them. They will linger in front of the sniper rifle for quite some time. Their suspicions will be justified. They'll talk amongst themselves about a purported assassination attempt. Their uncertainty